TIM MYERS'S LIGHTHOUSE MYSTERY
SERIES

"A thoroughly delightful and original series. Book me at
Hatteras West any day!"

—Tamar Myers,
author of *Gruel and Unusual Punishment*

"Myers cultivates the North Carolina scenery with aplomb
and shows a flair for character."

—*Fort Lauderdale Sun-Sentinel*

"Entertaining . . . authentic . . . fun . . . a wonderful regional
mystery that will have readers rebooking for future stays at
the Hatteras West Inn and Lighthouse."

—*BookBrowser*

"Tim Myers proves that he is no one-book wonder . . . A
shrewdly crafted puzzle."

—*Midwest Book Review*

"Colorful . . . picturesque . . . light and entertaining."

—*Harriet Klausner*

Lighthouse Inn Mysteries by Tim Myers

INNKEEPING WITH MURDER
RESERVATIONS FOR MURDER
MURDER CHECKS INN
ROOM FOR MURDER

Candlemaking Mysteries by Tim Myers

AT WICK'S END

AT
Wick's End

Tim Myers

BERKLEY PRIME CRIME, NEW YORK

This is a work of fiction. Names, characters, places, and incidents either are the product of the author's imagination or are used fictitiously, and any resemblance to actual persons, living or dead, business establishments, events, or locales is entirely coincidental.

AT WICK'S END

A Berkley Prime Crime Book / published by arrangement with the author

PRINTING HISTORY
Berkley Prime Crime edition / February 2004

For information address: The Berkley Publishing Group,
a division of Penguin Group (USA) Inc.,
375 Hudson Street, New York, New York 10014.

ISBN: 0-425-19460-4

Berkley Prime Crime Books are published
by The Berkley Publishing Group,
a division of Penguin Group (USA) Inc.,
375 Hudson Street, New York, New York 10014.
The name BERKLEY PRIME CRIME and the BERKLEY PRIME CRIME design are trademarks belonging to Penguin Group (USA) Inc.

PRINTED IN THE UNITED STATES OF AMERICA

10 9 8 7 6 5 4 3 2 1

For my editor, Kim Lionetti,
and my agent, John Talbot;
my partners in crime.

Prologue

BELLE Black realized she had to be careful when she confronted the murderer about to visit her candle shop, At Wick's End. To think that someone she knew was a killer made her blood freeze, and Belle was beginning to have second thoughts about her plan. Should she have asked for help, secured a witness to what she was about to do, or should she have done the sensible thing and called the sheriff's department so they could deal with this themselves? No, they never would've believed her anyway. And what if she was wrong? The whole town would hear about it and think she was going senile. She'd just handle this like she'd handled every other problem at her building complex, River's Edge, perched on the banks of the Gunpowder River in the North Carolina mountains. Belle felt the burning of her righteous indignation flare up at the thought of what had happened almost under her nose. She'd call the sheriff once she had the satisfaction of hearing the killer admit to the litany of sins she was about to unveil. There would be time enough for a formal confession to the police after that.

As the front door of her shop opened, the telltale chime announced that her visitor had finally arrived.

"SO I WAS right," she said as her suspect stepped out of the shadows to face her. "You murdered that poor man and then stole from him." The calm tone of her voice did nothing to reveal the hammering in her chest.

"I was under the distinct impression that you had more than a guess when you asked me to come here. You don't have proof of anything, do you?" There was no heat in the words, an absence of any emotion at all. Surprisingly, that chilled Belle's heart more than a stormy confrontation.

With firm resolve, Belle said, "I'm not guessing. I've got evidence."

"I can't imagine what you think you have."

Belle said, "How about one of the diamonds from the robbery?"

That earned a startled look from the accused. She continued, "You must have dropped it before you could hide them all, because you missed one. Aren't you worried about fingerprints?" She saw the killer's gaze dart around the candle shop, so she hastily added, "You'll never find where I've hidden it. It's safe right where it is." Was it, though? Had she been too clever, setting this confrontation up without any backup support? It was time to end this before something bad happened.

Belle said sternly, "Turn yourself in. Please. They'll go easier on you if you take responsibility for what you've done. It's the only way out for you."

"I can think of another," the voice said, spoken again with no emotion at all. "I'll find the diamond without your help."

As the killer stepped forward, Belle realized too late that she'd put too much faith in her belief that all of mankind was basically good, that there was no inherent evil, and that anyone would do the right thing, given the chance.

It was the last mistake she ever made.

* * *

AFTER THE MEDDLING old lady was dead, the scene was easily set in the storeroom to look like an accident. There were, after all, many ways a neck could be broken.

Most likely Belle wouldn't have kept the errant diamond in her shop; there were too many people in and out of At Wick's End every day. No, the evidence had to in her apartment upstairs. There was a key to her place behind the door in the candle shop office; it was the worst kept secret at River's Edge. And now it was time to recover the only thing that could link the crime with the killer.

One

"MR. Black, I'm sorry to say that I have some bad news for you."

I choked the telephone in my hand and tried to hide my impatience. "What other kind of news do lawyers ever have? And I told you before, my name's Harrison."

After we'd gone through the introductions and pleasantries, I'd waited for the real reason this man was calling me. I had a few leads to follow up in my sales territory, and times were lean at the moment. Okay, who was I trying to kid? I was broke because I was not entirely enamored with the prospect of peddling computers that weren't nearly as efficient or modern as our brochures proclaimed. I just couldn't bring myself to sell an inferior product to an unsuspecting public. It was time to try my hand at something else, a fact I'd realized some time ago. No job ever seemed to capture my interest long enough for me to get comfortable with it, and sales was turning out to be no different from hardware store clerk, copier repairman, dance instructor or house sitter.

And now I had a lawyer on the line. This just wasn't turning out to be my decade.

"Err, Harrison, I'm sorry to say that your aunt Belle Black has passed on."

"Great-aunt," I corrected automatically as I felt a sudden twist in my gut. That's exactly what Belle had been to me as I'd grown up, the greatest great-aunt a kid could wish for. She was the one who slipped me candy bars and folded fives on the side, the one who stood up for me when no one else would. It was always Belle's place I retreated to when I ran away from home.

And now she was gone.

I asked, "What happened? Was it her heart?" It suddenly hit me that I had no idea how old Belle really was. She'd seemed ancient to me as a kid, but it was a funny fact that middle age kept getting later and later in my mind as I approached it. I was on the left side of thirty, though just barely. Belle had to be creeping up on eighty, if she wasn't already there.

The attorney said, "No, I'm afraid it was an accident."

"Just don't tell me it happened in a car," I said. I'd lost both my parents on my twenty-first birthday to a drunk driver, the last birthday I ever celebrated or acknowledged.

"No, she fell off a ladder at her candlemaking shop."

I couldn't believe it. "What was she doing on a ladder at her age? No, never mind that, nobody has to tell me how stubborn she was." Though we'd lived just a few hours apart, I hadn't made any real effort to keep up with Belle since I'd been on my own. Even when I'd moved to Red Creek six months ago, a bustling little town just twenty minutes away, it hadn't increased the time we spent together. Belle and I stuck to our old habits. Once or twice a year we'd have lunch together, but otherwise we both led our own lives.

And now I regretted every opportunity I'd passed up over the years to see her.

"Mr. Black, there are important matters that need to be

discussed immediately. Can you come by my office in an hour?"

Suddenly following up those sales leads wasn't all that important. "Just tell me where you are and I'll be there."

After I hung up the telephone, I stared at a photograph on the small desk tucked into one corner of my cramped apartment. It was of Belle and me together taken twenty years before, my hand firmly in hers as we walked across a footbridge at the park.

And I felt the lightness of her touch all over again.

I decided to take a shower before keeping the appointment. Even as the spray washed away my tears as I mourned for her, I wished it could do something about scouring the heavy sadness in my heart.

THE ATTORNEY, LUCAS Young, turned out to be nothing like his voice. I'd imagined a tall lanky fellow with ruffled black hair when we'd talked on the telephone. Instead, what I found was a portly little man with a hairline receding faster than a snowman melting in the spring. At least the wisps of remaining hair still had a dark hue, so I hadn't been completely wrong.

"Harrison, again, please accepts my condolences."

"Thanks," I said as I took a seat across from his desk. I'd managed to pull myself together after an extended shower that had drained the last of the hot water from my tank. Drops took care of the redness in my eyes, but there was nothing that could disguise the sudden weariness that had overcome me. "What's so urgent? Do I need to make the arrangements for the funeral?"

"No, no," he waved a hand in the air as he studied the papers in front of him. "Your aunt, great-aunt," he corrected himself immediately, "took care of all that herself. She didn't want a fuss. The cremation's already taken place, and there will be no service of any kind, per her orders. I'm afraid she was most emphatic about that point."

"When did she die?" I asked.

"Sometime late Sunday evening. I'm afraid she wasn't discovered until Monday morning."

"And it took you a full day to call me?"

He said, "Please understand, this was your great-aunt's wish, not my whim. She was quite matter-of-fact making her arrangements. There was to be absolutely no fuss at all."

I had to smile, a reaction I was sure would make Young think I was some kind of ghoul, but I'd heard Belle expound on the pointlessness of funerals all my life, and I was glad she'd stuck to her guns to the end.

"So why am I here?" I asked.

"As her only living relative, you stand to inherit her entire estate," the lawyer said.

"I can't imagine Belle had all that much," I said, "and I certainly don't feel the need to discuss it right now."

The attorney held up one hand. "I understand, it's a natural reaction. However, your great-aunt," he looked pleased at remembering her correct title, "insisted we do this her way." At that, Young smiled gently. "She was quite a forceful lady."

"You don't have to tell me," I said. "Okay, what did Belle have to say?"

Young reached across his desk and handed me a letter. I felt a chill sweep over me as I recognized the precise, spiderweb writing. "Your great-aunt wanted you to read this. I'll give you some privacy," he added as he stood and excused himself from his office.

My hands trembled as I tore open the envelope, somehow uneasy with this missive from the grave.

I needn't have worried. Though Belle herself was gone, in this letter, at least, she was still with me, full of every bit of spit and vinegar as she'd ever been.

Harrison, my boy, if you're reading this, I've finally kicked the bucket. What a run I had! Don't mourn me, young man, and that's an order. I had more joy than sorrow, more smiles than frowns. It was a good solid life, one well worth living, but it's time for me to shuffle off.

You, on the other hand, are just getting started. I know, you don't feel all that young, but from where I'm sitting, you're still in short pants.

Let's cut to the chase, you know I never really liked all that sentimental mush. I'm giving you At Wick's End, and more importantly, all of River's Edge. You didn't know I owned the whole building, did you? The old girl still has a few surprises up her sleeve.

I put the letter down for a moment, astounded that Belle had been a property owner and landlord. So that was why she'd taken me on such an extensive tour of the converted factory and warehouse when she'd first told me of her plans to open a candle shop there. What had once been a huge expansive workspace on the banks of the Gunpowder River was now divided into stores, shops, offices and even an apartment where Belle lived. At Wick's End was in one corner of the downstairs space. I hadn't really understood her fascination with candles and had passed it off as some kind of hobby to keep her active in her later years.

I picked up the letter again and continued reading.

Now don't get too excited. River's Edge barely brings in enough to cover the taxes and monthly expenses, and you'll need to work hard to make a go of it. But that's exactly what I want you to do. At Wick's End is a wonderful place, and I want you to quit whatever dead-end job you're currently in and run my shop. Your shop now, actually. Candles bring light into the world, my boy, and we need all the illumination we can get.

Allow an old woman the last word. Throw yourself into this, Harrison, and make me proud.

I leaned back in my chair, clutching the letter tightly in my hands. Reading my great-aunt's words on paper brought her back to me, if only for a few moments, and I promised myself that I'd do my utmost to grant her last request. She didn't want me mourning her death. The best thing I could do was respect her wishes and get on with the business of living. But it appeared Belle was going to shake my life up more in her departure than she ever had when she'd been alive.

I CALLED MR. Young back in after I finished reading Belle's message for the third time.

He gestured to the letter. "I'm hoping she explained it all to you in there."

I shrugged. "I own River's Edge now, and she wants me to run the candle shop myself."

The attorney said, "That's the gist of it." He tapped a paper on his desk and added, "I'm afraid selling the property is out of the question. She's locked up the right to do that until you've operated the shop for five years."

"I had no intention of putting the place on the market," I said stiffly.

Mr. Young nodded. "I'm sure that's the case, but I wanted to clear that up from the outset. You should know what will happen if you decide candlemaking isn't for you. If you relinquish your rights before the five years are up, the property will be auctioned off to the highest bidder, with the proceeds going to your great-aunt's favorite charity. The same thing will happen if you should die before the deadline. So, are you ready?"

"For what? You said yourself there's not going to be a funeral."

The attorney shook his head. "I'm talking about the tour of your new property."

"We might as well get it over with," I said, wondering what I was getting myself into.

One thing was certain—it had to be better than selling second-rate computers. I hoped.

* * *

AS I STOOD in front studying the building, I had to admit, the converted warehouse was glorious. There was no doubt about that. River's Edge sported a long two-story facade of brick that looked every minute of its hundred years. A broad green awning covered the first-floor windows, supported by massive handmade oaken brackets from a timber-framer's dream, while the second-story windows were open and uncluttered as they looked out onto the Gunpowder River. A set of nine steps led down from the porch that spanned the front of the building all the way to the river, and I could see where a recent high water level had danced up to the fifth step. Old-fashioned iron lamps hung in front of every shop, and sets of oak doors guarded each store. There was an assortment of tables in front of a café, and a few matching benches spaced along some of the other storefronts.

It was hard to believe that it was suddenly all mine, mortgage and all.

Mr. Young stood beside me as I took in my new surroundings. "It's something, isn't it? Your great-aunt did a wonderful job holding it all together, no matter what the difficulties. Now where would you like to start?"

I gestured to the café, with its inviting bay windows and a welcoming sign that said, THE CROCKED POT in carefully carved wooden letters. "Let's get some coffee first, and then we can take the grand tour."

We walked in and found a cluster of folks gathered at one of the large tables in back. I was more interested in the architecture than the people at the moment, though. The dark hardwood floors, once scarred and stained from the hard work that had gone on there long before, were now polished to a high sheen, though the integrity of the old wood still shined through. The ceilings were a maze of exposed rafters, pipes and ducts, giving an urban, industrial feel to the place.

We approached the lady at the counter and I said, "We'd like two coffees, please."

The plus-size woman had gentle gray eyes, soft brown

curls and a disposition made for smiling. She laughed softly at my order. "Oh, you'll have to do better than that. We haven't served plain coffee here in donkey years." She gestured to the board behind her and it looked like Starbuck's had invaded.

Mr. Young said, "Allow me to make the introductions. Millie Nelson, this is Harrison Black. He's all that's left of Belle's family." What a way to introduce someone.

Millie came out from behind the counter, her smile gone as she took my hand in hers. "Of course. Harrison, I'm so sorry for your loss."

"Thanks, Ms. Nelson, I appreciate that."

"Please, call me Millie." She grabbed my arm and led me to the table where a group of people were clustered. "Everybody, this is Harrison Black. He was Belle's great-nephew."

"I don't know how great I was," I said with a slight smile, a joke that Belle and I had shared all our lives. Nobody at the table seemed to get it. So much for a good first impression.

Mr. Young stepped up and announced, "Harrison's more than Belle's kin. He's inherited River's Edge."

I looked around the table, trying to conjure up my best smile as Millie introduced me to them.

As she gestured to a thin young blonde dressed in a billowing tie-dyed dress, Millie said, "This is Heather Bane. She owns The New Age." I nodded, and Heather returned my greeting in like fashion. "Next, there's Pearly Gray, he's the general handyman around here."

Pearly, an older fellow with a head of hair that matched his name, shook my hand hard enough to nearly break it. "Good to meet you, Harrison. Sorry about Belle. She will be truly missed."

The handyman's voice was rich and cultured as the words flowed from his lips.

"Thanks. Man, you must have had a tough time growing up with a name like Pearly." Too late I realized that I probably should have thought before I spoke, but Pearly just laughed.

"My real given name is Parsons, but I seem to have acquired the name Pearly as the luster of my hair started to fade. It's actually the name I prefer now."

"Pearly it is," I said.

Millie next turned to a man nattily dressed in a three-piece, charcoal-gray suit with a Phi Beta Kappa key hanging down from his vest and said more formally, "May I present Gary Cragg, our resident attorney."

Cragg shook my hand as he nodded to Mr. Young. "Delighted. Now if you'll excuse me, I'm due in court soon." He was nearly to the door when he turned and said, "We need to speak later, Mr. Black. There are things most urgent we must discuss."

"I'll be here," I said to his departing back.

Millie turned to the last woman still without an introduction.

"And finally, Harrison, I'd like you to meet Eve Pleasants. She worked with Belle."

As I offered Eve my hand, she looked at it as if it were contaminated, then said gruffly, "If you'll excuse me, it's time to open the shop."

I said, "That's a great idea. I can't wait to get started."

Eve shot me a withering glare as she said, "I'm perfectly capable of running the candle shop without your uh . . . assistance. Why don't you finish your tour?"

There was nothing welcoming in her words at all, but I decided to deal with that later. "Thanks, I appreciate that. As soon as I get settled in, I'll be over."

As she huffed off, Millie said softly, "Don't take it personally, Harrison. She and your great-aunt were quite close."

"To be honest with you, I'm glad to know someone misses her," I said.

Millie patted my shoulder as she said, "Oh, she's missed all right, but the show must go on and our stores have to open. Belle was most clear about that, she left letters for each of us. Now let me get you that coffee. What kind would you like?"

Her smile was infectious. "Surprise me."

She nodded as Mr. Young touched my arm. "We need to go upstairs and start our tour."

"Coffee first," I said. Millie declined my offered payment, then Mr. Young and I ascended the stairs to the second floor. He said, "The tenants with storefront shops have the lower level, while the upper area is reserved for businesses and your residence."

"I had no idea the place was so big," I said as I studied the second-floor directory.

"Oh, yes, Belle did her best to keep the building occupied at full capacity. That's odd," he said as we entered the hallway.

"What's wrong?" I asked.

He gestured to the door at the end of the hall and said, "That's Belle's apartment. I inventoried her belongings earlier this morning, and that door was firmly locked when I left it."

I looked closer at the door in question and saw that it was pushed open a few inches, as if someone had been in too big a hurry to shut it behind them.

Two

As I started toward the door, Mr. Young touched my arm. He said, "Shouldn't we call the police and let them investigate this?"

"If you'd feel better staying out here, you're welcome to do just that, but I'm going in."

He didn't have much choice after that but to follow me in.

Someone had wrecked the place, tearing books from the shelves and dumping every drawer in the apartment. I spotted a two-foot-tall candle lying on its side and picked it up, since it was the closest thing there was to a weapon in sight. I couldn't believe how heavy it was in my hands.

There was no need for defense, though. There wasn't a soul around.

"I take it the apartment wasn't like this when you left it this morning," I said as I surveyed the damage.

"I assure you, it was in pristine condition," Mr. Young said. "I'm sorry, but we simply must call the police now."

"Fine by me," I said, "but I don't even know if anything's been taken. You said you just did an inventory. Why don't you take a few minutes after you call and see if anything's missing?"

Mr. Young nodded, and after he telephoned the police, he took a quick survey of the place. As he scanned the mess, I picked up a photograph lying facedown on the floor. The glass had been broken in the frame, but the picture itself was unharmed. It could have been the static electricity in the air, but I felt a shock as my fingertips touched it, a framed copy of the photograph I'd been looking at earlier that morning of Belle and me together. I felt a lump forming in my throat, and barely heard Mr. Young's next comment.

"I don't understand this. Nothing of value seems to be missing."

Seeing her things violated like that appalled me. I waited until I couldn't take it anymore. It was obvious we were a low priority for the police. I said, "Listen, do you mind hanging around here and taking care of this? I need to get down to the candle shop."

"You really should stay for the police," Mr. Young said in an officious manner.

"What can I tell them that you can't? This is the first time I'm seeing this place. You can tell them what it was like when you left. If they decide they need to talk to me, send them down to the shop. I'm not going anywhere." I'd deal with the disaster at Belle's place later. For now, I just had to get out of there.

As I hurried downstairs, I couldn't help wondering what the thief had been looking for, though. And more importantly, had they found it, or was there still something they wanted hidden in Belle's room?

EVE WAS RINGING up a customer's order as I walked in, so I decided to start my tour of Wick's End without her. The main body of the shop was divided into two spaces, with the lion's share taken up by row upon row of shelves sporting waxes, wicks, molds, racks of tools, boilers, pots, and vials of oddly-colored potions. There were powders, decals, globs of weird gels and sheets of honeycombed wax dyed in hues that rainbows hadn't even dreamed of. But most of all, there were candles.

Short and fat, long and tapered to slender points, round candles, candles in jars, in mugs and even in small teakettles. There were candles with twists and braids that belonged in a Salvador Dali painting or an Edgar Allan Poe nightmare, candles that floated in water and some that seemed to be a part of the water itself.

Eve found me gawking at the array after her customer left.

"I've got to tell you," I said, "I never imagined there were this many different types of candles on Earth."

She tried to hide her satisfaction with the compliment. "We don't have a tenth of the candles that we make on display right now. In fact, our inventory's been dropping recently."

"Any reason in particular?" I asked.

She didn't want to answer, that much was obvious, but finally Eve shrugged and explained, "Belle's been too distracted to do much original work lately. You know about the offer, don't you?" Before I could say a word, Eve said heatedly, "You can't sell River's Edge, Mr. Black. This was Belle's home."

"I have no intention of selling," I said, neglecting to mention that Mr. Young had already informed me that it wasn't an option.

Eve said, "Do you mean that?"

"I'd like things to stay just the way they are around here, at least for now. I'm smart enough to realize that I don't know enough at this point to decide what changes might need to be made, but I'm staying."

"I can't tell you what a burden you've lifted from me. I naturally assumed that from the moment I found Belle on the floor that the building would be sold. It's callous to think that way about a friend's passing, and she was my friend, believe me, but I don't know what I'd do without At Wick's End in my life."

"You don't have to worry about that," I said. "Tell me about how you found Belle."

I spotted a lone tear creeping down her cheek. "Must I? I've been trying to forget the sight ever since I found her. There was simply no sense in it. I'm no spring chicken, you can be assured of that, but I didn't mind in the least going up and down ladders around here, and she was never shy about asking me to do so. I don't know if you're aware of it, but Belle grew to hate heights over the last few months. Why, it even made her nervous living on the second floor, and she was surrounded by all that mortar and brick up there."

"So what could have possessed her to climb a ladder in the storeroom?"

Eve wrung her hands together. "That's what I don't understand. There was a box of golden beeswax sheets near her body on the floor, but when I checked the shelves out front we had plenty! It just doesn't make sense." As she said the last word, she began to cry in earnest.

I never know what to do in those situations. We had just met, so I couldn't very well offer her an embrace unless she initiated it. Nor did I feel comfortable just standing there until she cried it out of her system. I finally settled for touching her shoulder lightly. "It's probably too soon for you to be working," I said. "Why don't you go home and I'll take care of the shop myself."

She swabbed at her damp cheeks and said through the snuffles, "You must think I'm a fragile old woman, falling apart like this. I'm so sorry."

"What I think is that you just lost a very dear friend," I said gently.

"Thank you for that, Mr. Black," as she touched my hand.

"It's Harrison," I said.

"Not Harry for short," Eve said, trying to lighten the gloom in the air.

I smiled. "You can call me whatever you want to, but Harrison's the only name I'll answer to."

She nodded. "Harrison it is." As she wiped the last tear from her face, she said, "Why don't we get started."

"What are we going to do?" I asked, suddenly curious about this turnaround in her behavior.

"Why, I'm going to teach you all there is to know about making candles," she said as she headed for the back room. "Give me a minute to get things set up. Just keep an eye on the front door. If anybody comes in, call me."

I WAS STANDING by the display of books on candlemaking that we stocked, selecting a copy of each for my supplemental education, when the bell over the front door chimed.

An older woman walked into the store, draped in fur and the smell of money. "May I help you?" I asked, hoping she knew what she needed, since I wouldn't have a clue to the answer of the most basic of questions.

"I'm here to see the proprietor," she said airily.

"You've found him," I said. "What can I do for you?"

"I was passing by and saw the wonderful display of candles you have here. I understand this is a place for instruction as well as purchasing, is that correct?"

"Yes, ma'am," I said.

"Very well, I'd like to learn to create my own candles. It's always best to start at the beginning. After all, one must have a foundation in the basics before one's imagination can take control. Are you free for instruction now? I have some time available."

"I'm sorry, but my schedule's pretty full at the moment," I said. I wasn't about to admit that the only thing I knew about candles was how to burn them. "However," I added, "we've got a woman on staff here who is most adept at candlemaking, and I'm sure she would be glad to help you today."

Her gaze tightened slightly. "What is your name, sir?"

I gave her my name, and she said, "Mr. Black, I work with proprietors, not with their staff."

"I could try to work you in, but I'm not making any

promises," I said, hoping she'd take the hint and allow Eve to teach her.

The woman looked at me steadily for a few seconds that felt like days. "As I said, I expect the owner to assist me. I suggest you find the time for me. I trust you'll be able to give me an hour on Thursday. Let's say ten o'clock, shall we?" She handed me an elegantly printed card as she left. I hadn't lied to her, but I wasn't about to confess that I was the rankest amateur either.

Eve was standing in the wings. "Harrison, if you don't mind my saying so, you're going to need to work on your people skills if you're going to run At Wick's End. That woman was ready to spend a fortune, and those customers are rare enough to be treated like royalty when they come in."

I studied the card. *Mrs. Henrietta Jorgenson* was all it said, in raised letters that looked handcrafted. "Can you believe this? She actually gave me one of her calling cards."

Eve asked for the card, and I handed it over. She said, "Mrs. Jorgenson! She's a legend around here in the craft circles. Wilma Martin runs the needlepoint store in Three Corners. She told me one time Mrs. Jorgenson paid for her Alaskan cruise with two purchases from her shop! Belle and I used to dream about her coming by At Wick's End."

"So all our money problems are over," I said, feeling slightly better about the payments looming over my head.

Eve frowned for a moment, then said, "Not necessarily. Anne Green at Crewel World said something to offend her, quite by accident, I'm certain, and suddenly Anne was blacklisted at all the craft shows. It nearly put her out of business. So what did Her Highness say?"

"She wants me to teach her how to make candles," I said. "And she wants to start Thursday."

Eve looked grim as she said, "Then you'd better get your first lesson right away."

WE MOVED TO the smaller working area in the back where it was obvious the regular classes were taught. There were six benches around the room, with enough space for twenty-four students. Sinks and storage took up the rest of the tight quarters. I picked up a chunk of translucent wax and said, "Let's get started."

Eve took it from me and put the wax back on the counter. "We don't have time to go into dipping or pouring just yet. Hmmm, I suppose sheet rolling would be the best place to start. Let me collect some materials and we can get started."

I followed her to one of the shelves near the front and saw an array of honeycombed sheets in a variety of hues, along with wicks, knives, straight edges and cookie cutters. She chose a packet with sheets of golden-yellow wax a little narrower than a piece of notebook paper but quite a bit longer. I picked up a pack myself so I could get a closer look. The wax had a definite raised imprint throughout. "This is neat. It's like a soccer ball."

Eve took the packet from my hand and said, "It's a hive pattern. We only need one for now," she added as she returned mine to the shelf behind her.

Eve motioned me to one of the workbenches, a long countertop with overhead lights that illuminated the entire tabletop. After she removed the wax and wicks from the pack, I grabbed the sheet and flexed it in my hands. "It's kind of thick, isn't it?"

Eve shook her head and easily located a seam I'd missed. She peeled one sheet from the other and handed it to me. I was expecting it to be sticky for some odd reason, but it wasn't at all. The single sheet was really pliable as I made waves with it, shifting it in my hands. I held it to my nose and caught a pleasant, faint scent that did indeed remind me of honey.

I caught Eve smiling at me, something she quickly stifled the second she saw me notice. "Here's the wick we'll be using," she said as she handed me a piece of string that was thicker than kite string but thinner than a shoelace.

"It's pretty long, isn't it?" I asked.

She said, "We can cut it to any length we need. Now today is rather warm, so we can skip the preheating process.

Sometimes in winter I like to use a blow-dryer to make the wax more malleable."

"Blow-dryer. Got it," I said as I fiddled with the wax. "What do I do now?"

"Lay the sheet out flat," she said. "Then trim the wick within three-fourths of an inch beyond the edge of the wax. No, not that way, go along the width, not the length."

I did as I was told, and she continued. "Now fold the wax over the wick tightly. Don't be afraid to use your thumbnail to clinch it into place along the entire length. Remember, the tighter the candle is rolled, the better and longer it will burn."

I finished that step, and she reluctantly nodded after inspecting my work and adding an extra pinch or two. "Now it's simply a matter of rolling the candle up tightly till you get to the end."

I did as I was instructed, amazed at how simple the process was. Until I found that somehow I'd gotten off course and my candle now had a definite diagonal slant to it. "Okay, how do I fix this?"

"You rolled your candle too quickly. Unroll it, the wax is very forgiving, and try it again. Take your time and watch the edges."

It was just like unraveling paper towels from the roll as I started over at the cinched wick. This time I was more careful with the edges and produced what I thought was a decent candle.

"What do you think?" I asked as I gave it to Eve.

"It's adequate for a first try. You'll get better as you practice. If this were a regular class, we'd dip the tip and butt of the candle in melted beeswax, but it's not necessary right now." She unrolled the candle, handed the sheet and wick back to me, and said, "Now let's try that again."

By the time I'd finished my fourth try, I was really starting to enjoy the process. "Hey, this is fun," I said as I laid the finished candle down.

Eve said, "I believe you've got the hang of it now. This is the simplest form of candlemaking we teach. Now we can move on to shaping unique candles with the sheets of wax. Mrs. Jorgenson will want to be able to do that, I'm sure."

Eve was just starting the next lesson when the door chime announced another customer. "That will have to do for now," she said. "We've still got a shop to run, you know."

I wanted to follow her out and observe, but Eve said, "Practice makes perfect, Harrison."

So I went back to my wax and started a brand-new candle. I was beginning to see why Belle had gotten hooked. Candlemaking could be a lot of fun.

AFTER I'D ROLLED and rerolled candles more times than I could count, I was ready for a break. Eve was involved in a deep discussion with one of our customers about the advantages of pellets versus blocks, a conversation that went entirely over my head. I waved to her, said I'd be back soon, and decided it was time for another cup of Millie's coffee. If I was lucky, maybe I'd get a dollop of insight about what really went on around River's Edge too. I had a feeling that if anyone had her finger on the pulse of the place, it would be the owner of The Crocked Pot.

I was just leaving the shop when a uniformed police officer walked up. "Are you Harrison Black?" he asked in a deep baritone.

"I am," I admitted. "I assume you're here about the robbery. Where did Mr. Young go?"

"He had to get back to his office, but not before he assured me that nothing had been taken. Pardon my saying so, but there's not much there worth stealing. It could just be that the thief tore up the place out of frustration. That would explain the mess."

"I don't buy that for a second," I said. "Nobody's going to walk up to the only apartment on the second floor of this building and break in on a whim. Whoever did this was after something."

The officer shrugged. "I can pass your concerns on to the sheriff, but there's really nothing else I can do here."

"Thanks for coming by," I said, trying to keep the disappointment out of my voice.

The officer must have caught it, though. "I'd honestly spend more time on this if anything of value was missing, but we've just had a homicide committed during a jewelry store robbery and we're working on it with every free man-hour."

"I heard about it on the news. The store owner was the one killed in the robbery, wasn't he?"

"That's why we're giving it so much attention. There was half a million dollars in diamonds taken. Don't worry, we'll catch them soon enough."

"And I'm left to my own devices. I understand perfectly."

The cop looked at me a second more, tipped his hat and walked to his squad car.

It appeared that Belle's break-in wasn't going to be a high priority for the local police.

I'd just have to solve that particular mystery myself.

Three

"THIS one's on the house too," Millie said as she slid a cup of coffee across the counter to me. "Having to deal with Belle's death, your inheritance, and a break-in all in the same day is too much to expect of anybody."

"How did you know about the break-in?" I asked as I sipped the coffee. It had a nutty taste that startled me at first, but it quickly grew on me.

Millie laughed as she took a swipe at the counter. "Oh please, Harrison, I knew what happened long before the squad car showed up. There's something you should know—River's Edge is a great deal like its own small town. It's hard not to know what's going on in other people's lives around here. With one obvious exception." She hesitated, towel in hand.

"I'm waiting," I said after taking another sip. "You can't leave me hanging like that."

Millie said, "I really shouldn't be starting rumors. You'll find out soon enough yourself."

I said, "Millie, I'm counting on you to keep me informed around here."

She snapped, "And what exactly gave you the impression that I'm such a busybody?"

Oh, no, I'd put my foot in it again. "I don't think that at all. It just seems to me that The Crocked Pot is a gathering place for everybody around here. Sorry if I offended you."

She shook her head and laughed softly. "George, that's my husband, says the same thing. I guess I'm a little touchy about it is all."

"What does George do?" I asked, hoping to make her forget what I'd said.

"What doesn't he do, I like to say. He's a volunteer fireman, he's a lay reader at St. Albans and he helps out at the animal shelter. Whenever he's not volunteering, he manages to make custom furniture for the high-end marketplace."

"Wow, when does he have time for you?"

Millie smiled. "I may have just one job, but it manages to fill my time. Don't you worry about George and me, we do just fine."

Millie's gaze drifted upstairs, then returned to me. She said softly, "Harrison, I shouldn't have said anything, but since I started it, I feel obliged to finish. If I were you I'd keep my eye on Gary Cragg. He's up to something, but I can't for the life of me figure out what it is. There's one thing I can tell you, though. He and Belle had a major problem with each other lately."

"Do you have any idea what it was about?" I asked.

She said, "I asked Belle about it last week, but she just mumbled something about sharks and wouldn't say another word. There aren't any in the river out there, but I'm not so sure we don't have a couple at River's Edge."

"Who else should I watch out for?" I asked.

"There's a fellow Belle just rented space to upstairs named Markum. I don't know if that's his first name or last, since he's the only tenant who's never set foot in my place."

"What does he do?" I asked after finishing off the coffee.

"The sign on his door says, 'Salvage and Recovery', whatever that's supposed to mean. If he runs a junkyard, it's not around here. I understand he and Belle had words the other day." She took my cup and refilled it. "Never mind, he's probably fine. George says I have too much time on my hands between my breakfast and lunch rush hours, and I'll never admit it to his face, but most likely he's right." She studied me a second, then asked, "So how are you and Eve getting along?"

"Well, she's teaching me candlemaking basics, if that means anything."

Millie smiled. "You can bet your life it does. Eve's a candle fanatic. She wouldn't teach you if she didn't like you, Harrison. You two should be just fine."

I could still remember the tone of her critiques of my early efforts. "If you say so."

She flipped the towel gently at me. "Trust me on that, Harrison. Now if you'll excuse me, I've got a batch of blueberry doughnuts to mix up for tomorrow morning. Want me to save you a couple?"

"That would be great. Thanks."

"It's all part of The Crocked Pot's service, sir."

I decided it would be a good time to tackle Belle's apartment. Eve could handle At Wick's End by herself. Truth be told, she'd most likely do better solo until I learned enough to help out in the shop. Cleaning up the mess at Belle's place wouldn't get any easier, and the longer I put it off, the harder it would be.

I was just about to reach the door upstairs when I heard someone moving around inside.

I didn't even have the heavy candle to defend myself, but I charged in anyway.

It was time to find out who was breaking in, and what they wanted from Belle, once and for all.

I was startled to find Heather Bane from The New Age shop putting Belle's clothes in a box that had once held a case of Maker's Mark whiskey.

I said, "What are you doing in here?"

She looked startled by my sudden appearance. Perhaps even a little guilty.

"I heard about the break-in, and I couldn't bear the thought of you tackling this mess by yourself, not with what you've been through."

"That was thoughtful of you," I said, trying to keep the accusation out of my voice. "How did you happen to get in? I was under the impression this door locked automatically." That was something Mr. Young had shown me himself soon after we'd discovered the break-in.

"Well, it wasn't locked when I got here. In fact, I was kind of surprised to find the door wide open. Harrison, I should have asked you for your permission to do this first, shouldn't I? I can't help myself, I just get an impulse and go with it. That's how I got my shop, you know."

She continued working, stowing things from the floor in boxes as she talked, and I found myself joining her. At least I could keep an eye on her that way, and the work had to be done before I could move in. "I'd like to hear the story," I said as I folded some of Belle's sweaters and put them in a nearby box.

Heather said, "One day I was canoeing on the Gunpowder and saw River's Edge for the first time. The building was so cool, and I'd been looking for something to do with my inheritance." She paused, then said, "I'm not rich or anything, but my grandmother died and left me some money. Only thing was, there was a catch. I had to start a business and run it, or the money would go to my sister. She's the sensible one, or so everybody thinks. Grams was always concerned that my life was without direction, so I took a deep breath and rented my space. I've always been fascinated with crystals and the power stones have to heal, so naturally that's the kind of store I wanted. When you get the chance, I'd love to give you the grand tour."

"I'd like that," I said as the last of Belle's clothes went into the boxes. Most likely this young woman was harmless and my suspicious mind was just working overtime.

Heather said, "Okay, you've got clothes in these four boxes, and miscellaneous stuff in these two. Would you like me to take the ones with Belle's clothes to the Salvation Army? A lot of her things are too nice to just throw out."

Something gnawed at the edge of my mind. Had Heather actually been trying to help, or had she come back for what she'd missed earlier? What better excuse to show up again than to say she was cleaning up the earlier mess made in her search? And what was really in those boxes? I just couldn't take the chance, no matter how benign it all seemed.

"Tell you what," I said, "I'll take them later myself."

"I don't mind," she insisted. "The drop-off is right on my way home."

I took the box that was in her hands and said firmly, "I appreciate the offer, I truly do, but there are a few things that have great sentimental value I may want to keep as a remembrance. Thanks again, though."

Heather tried to hide her disappointment. "Okay. If that's all then, I'd better get back downstairs and close up my shop."

"You didn't leave it open the entire time you were up here, did you?"

"Yes, but I've got a woman helping me who comes in three afternoons a week and works the occasional full day to give me a break. Mrs. Quimby is a godsend. Don't forget, you've got one deluxe tour coming any time you want it."

"I won't forget," I said as I tried to see if Heather was leaving with more than she had had when she arrived. It was impossible to tell under her baggy outfit, but I doubted she'd had the chance to take anything yet. After all, it was obvious she had expected to leave with those boxes long before I ever showed up at Belle's apartment.

I DON'T KNOW what I was expecting to find in the boxes: jewelry, cash or something. All I could come up with was a quarter that must have slipped out of one of Belle's pockets, and a broach that was obviously costume jewelry. It was looking more and more like Heather had been the Good Samaritan she claimed to be after all.

Unless she had indeed managed to walk off with something I hadn't seen.

There was yet a third possibility. I might have interrupted her second search before she'd had the chance to find her bounty.

I wasn't about to give her or anyone else another chance. I picked up the telephone book and called a locksmith.

There was no way I was going to sleep in that apartment until I had a brand-new lock in place, and the only key to it.

GOING THROUGH SOME of the other boxes as I waited for the locksmith, I found the two-foot candle I'd picked up earlier to defend myself and decided it was one worth keeping. I don't know what made me do it, but I put it on the countertop at the bar and lit it with an igniter I found in one of the drawers. Ordinarily I wasn't a big fan of scents in candles, but this one had an aroma of cinnamon that made me think of Snickerdoodle cookies, a treat Belle had baked for me as a kid. I decided to burn it an hour a night in honor of Belle, my own tribute to her. As the wick took life, I found myself finally beginning to experience the grief of losing her. Delayed reaction, I guess. A tear ran down my cheek and struck the flame. It wasn't enough to put the fire out, but it did cause it to sputter for a moment before jumping back to life.

It was as if Belle herself was telling me not to waste any tears on her. The words of her letter echoed in my mind again, and I decided this simple tribute was more in order for a life well led than any service or eulogy.

It was the best way to say good-bye I could imagine.

IT'S ALWAYS HARD for me to sleep in strange places, and there were few stranger than the second floor of River's

Edge when the complex was deserted. I tossed and turned until I finally tired of fighting it. Instead of lying there with my eyes wide open staring at the ceiling, I decided it might be a good time to do a little more exploring in the candle shop downstairs. There was one thing to be said for Belle's arrangement: it certainly made commuting between work and home easier. As I walked outside to get into the shop, I saw a brief flash of light in the distance, accompanied by a muted rumbling, but it was too far away to matter to me. I had work to do. I had my key in the store's front door lock when movement caught my attention out of the corner of my eye. The bushes near the building shook slightly, and I wondered if it was just the wind, or perhaps something more ominous.

"Who's there?" I called out into the night.

There was no answer, and I thought about checking it out more thoroughly, but the darkness was getting to me. I decided the best place for me to be was on the other side of that locked door. I didn't really breathe again until I was safely inside. No doubt it had just been my imagination, but I still felt better with all the lights of the shop blazing.

I was so lost in the world of candles in At Wick's End that the storm was on me before I realized what was happening. There was a flash of light, followed almost immediately by the crack of thunder, and instantly I was plunged into darkness.

River's Edge was without power, and I was alone in a strange place in complete and utter blackness.

Right on its heels, another explosion of lightning ripped through the night, blinding me for an instant as the candle-making shop was bathed in sudden white light. I remembered seeing boxes of decorative matches near the cash register, so I felt my way toward it between flashes of lightning. Outside, the rain was drumming against the windows like fists hammering urgently to get in. I struck a match and followed its brief light to the display candles up front. Grabbing the nearest twisted taper, I lit it, feeling instantly better now that I had my own source of light. It was amazing how much illumination it offered. The flickering flame from the candle in my hand was no match for the next burst of lightning though. As the brutal force of the flash vanished, it was followed almost instantly by a thundering roar that shook me so violently I nearly dropped the candle. I could smell the burning ozone in the air as I fought to get my sight back.

My eyes were just starting to clear when another flash of lightning blasted into the room.

Even worse luck, I happened to be looking toward one of the bay windows in front of the candleshop. The lightning strike was like a blow to the chest, driving me back against a display bench, and extinguishing the candle in my grasp.

But it wasn't just the harshness of the explosion that made me stumble backward. There, by the window, was a bloodless white face peering in at me.

I DROPPED THE candle as my back hit a display shelf, my sight lost again from the flash of lightning. The man outside beat on the window and yelled, "Open up," as I scrambled blindly for the beeswax candle. I finally chased it down under one of the shelves. That's the problem with cylindrical objects; they have a tendency to roll. Just as I started to light the wick again, the power came back on.

The ghostly face I'd seen was clear now with illumination. Standing outside the shop was a man in uniform, soaked to the bone, with one of the palest complexions I'd ever seen in my life. He flashed a badge and repeated his command to open up.

I did so, but not before grabbing a hand-forged iron candle stand that would do in a pinch as a weapon.

"I'm one soaked rat," the cop said as he walked in, shaking the water from his jacket and running his fingers through his hair. "The rain's coming down so hard and blowing in under the awning I didn't have a chance." He noticed the stand in my hand and added, "Plan on clubbing a cop, are you?"

"Do you mind if I have another look at that badge?"

He grinned, a reaction that surprised me. "Don't mind a bit. Listen, I hate to leave puddles all over your store, Belle would have shot me. How about getting me a towel from the bathroom? She keeps extras on the shelf above the mirror."

I glanced at his badge, then retrieved a towel. Man, I was getting too paranoid for my own good. First, the wind had rustled through the bushes, then that storm really had given me the creeps. Seeing the sheriff's pale face lurking in the window hadn't helped matters.

As he dried off, the sheriff said, "My name's Coburn. You must be Harrison. Belle told me a lot about you. She was a truly fine lady."

I nodded. "I think so too. Did you come to investigate the break-in upstairs?"

Coburn shook his head, drying some of the moisture from his hair. "I thought Stevens took care of that."

"He seemed to think it was some random act of violence," I said.

"And you believe differently," he said flatly.

"Think about it. Whoever broke in had to have had a key. There was no sign that the lock had been forced, and Lucas Young swears he locked the door behind him when he came by to do his inventory this morning. The lock worked fine too, I tested it myself after everyone else was gone. And another thing, what thief in his right mind would randomly break into an apartment on the second floor of a building like this? It just doesn't make sense."

"So your instincts are better than my man's," he said evenly. "Mind if I ask what qualifications you've got?"

I debated telling him I'd cut my teeth on Agatha Christie, and had continued my love affair with mysteries ever since. I figured out the killer more times than not in just about every book I read, but I doubted it would carry much weight with him. "Common sense. I tried to tell your man that, but he seemed more concerned with your jewelry store robbery."

The sheriff stopped toweling his hair for a moment as he

gave me a solid stare. "The robbery's nothing, as far as I'm concerned. It's the murder that's got my blood boiling. I take it personally when somebody dies in my jurisdiction."

Okay, I had to admit he had a point. "I understand that, but I still don't like the idea of somebody breaking in Belle's place, no matter what your deputy thinks happened."

Coburn said, "I read the report. Like you said, there was no sign of forced entry, so the door was either unlocked when the thief got there, or whoever was up there had a key. Either way, that problem should be over now that you have a new lock on the apartment door."

"How did you know that?" I asked.

"I was playing chess with Christine Lanina when you called her. Christine's not just a good locksmith, she's a fine chess player. Blast it all, I thought I had her last move figured out, but she managed to come up with something new, so now I'm stuck again."

I took the offered towel back from him, considerably wetter now, and said, "Thanks for explaining how you knew about the new lock. I was beginning to think everybody in Micah's Ridge knew what I was up to."

He laughed, but there wasn't a great deal of humor in it. "Don't kid yourself, Harrison, everybody most likely does. You lived in big cities too long. It sounds like you've forgotten what it's like to live in a small town."

A thought suddenly struck me. "So if you're not here about the burglary, why did you come out here on a night like this?"

He shrugged. "Belle didn't believe in funerals, so there was no real way for me to say good-bye. I argued with her till I was blue in the face that the funeral wouldn't have been for her at all. It's a way for folks to deal with their loss, you know what I mean?" He studied his hands a moment, then added, "Anyway, I drove out here because I miss her. You have my condolences. The world's a little darker without her in it."

I took his hand, surprised by the gesture and the softness in his voice. "Thanks, I appreciate that. I miss her too."

Coburn glanced outside, and for the first time I noticed that the storm had abated during our conversation. He followed my gaze and said, "It's just drizzling now. I'd better get on home." The sheriff started for the door, then added, "You're working pretty late yourself, aren't you?"

"I couldn't sleep," I admitted.

Coburn nodded. "Lot of that going around these days." He took a card from his wallet and handed it to me. "Anything else comes up, you call me."

I took the card. "Thanks. I appreciate that."

After he was gone, I turned off the lights and locked up the store.

The storm had been a release for me, a purging. My jumpiness earlier was now gone. The intensity of the lightning barrage, and then the sight of what had looked like a corpse outside my window had buried me in a wash of adrenaline. Suddenly, I was so tired I barely made it up the stairs back to my apartment, and to my great surprise, sleep came easily after all.

Four

"**M**ILLIE, these are the best doughnuts I've ever had in my life, blueberry or otherwise," I said as I finished the third on my plate at The Crocked Pot the next morning. There were quite a few people there, no doubt due to Millie's fine offerings. She'd saved me two, and I'd added a third myself from the quickly-dwindling stack under glass on the counter. I was in the habit of walking in the evenings for exercise at my old apartment, something I was going to have to start again if I was going to be able to keep fitting into my clothes. I've got a weakness for the taste and aroma of freshly baked goodies, and I could see my relationship with Millie was going to be trying, a constant battle with temptation. This time temptation won, hands down.

"That's a real compliment," she said. "Are you sure you won't have another?"

I patted my stomach. "Not if I'm going to be able to fit through the door of At Wick's End."

I was just tossing my paper plate in the trash can when Gary Cragg, the attorney from upstairs, came in. "Mr. Black, I need a moment of your time."

"That's about all I can give you," I said. "I've got to move my things to River's Edge before we open the candle shop this morning." In truth, I knew I should have moved the day before, or even slept in my old apartment until I could get settled at Belle's, but I hadn't been up to tackling it after the day I'd had. I had to admit, it would feel more comforting having my own things around me again. I hadn't minded using Belle's shampoo, though I did smell faintly of apricots now, but I drew the line at borrowing her razor, and the stubble on my chin was starting to bother me.

Cragg looked around at the customers enjoying Millie's breakfast offerings. "I'll take whatever time you can give me, but I'd much rather speak with you in private. Why don't we go up to my office?"

"Walking up and down the stairs would burn all the time I've got." I thought about it a second, then suggested, "I can give you a minute outside on the front steps. Otherwise, it will have to wait until tonight." I was pushing my luck as it was, planning to pack my meager belongings, move them to River's Edge and still have time to prep myself for the next day's candlemaking lesson with Mrs. Jorgenson. Eve had been emphatic that I get in more practice rolling candles before I tackled the important private lesson with the woman who could make or break us.

Cragg glanced at his watch. "We can't do this in a minute or two. I'm free after five. We'll meet in my office then."

With that, he dismissed me, but I didn't have time to come up with something snappy to say in response. I've been known to have a slight problem with authority figures in the past, so I didn't take too kindly to the order implicit in his request, especially since he was my tenant, and not the other way around.

Maybe I'd show up at five, and maybe I wouldn't.

At the moment, I had some packing to do.

IT WAS AMAZING how little I'd acquired in the way of possessions over the years. After packing two boxes of keepsakes, a suitcase and travel bag stuffed with clothes, I was ready to move. I tossed out some things in my refrigerator that had been in there so long they were taking on lives of their own and grabbed a stack of paperbacks and magazines I'd already read to give to Mrs. Harper, the sweet old gal who lived next door. We often made it a habit of swapping reading materials. She had the most eclectic tastes of anybody I'd ever known, and a mind that had sharpened to a fine point over the years from her constant reading.

After I brought her up-to-date on my vastly changed life, she said, "I hate to see you go, Harrison. I'm going to miss you."

As I handed her my ragtag collection of reading materials, I said, "I'll miss you too, but I can't stay. It just makes sense this way now that I've got an apartment over the candle shop. Don't worry, I'll come see you when I get the chance."

"I might just surprise you," she said with a twinkle in her eye. "I've always been quite fond of candles. I may just come visit you at your store sometime soon."

"That would be great. Just give me time to get settled in first."

She smiled softly, "And wait until you learn how to make candles as well?" She patted my hand. "Don't worry. You'll do fine, Harrison."

"Thank you, ma'am."

She surprised us both by kissing me on the cheek just before saying good-bye.

And that was that, the final tie I had to my old life. At least it was near the end of the month, so I didn't waste much on unused rent. The landlord took my key, shrugged but otherwise showed no sign that my presence would be missed.

I loaded everything in the back of my pickup and I was on my way to my new home.

*   *   *

"GOOD MORNING," I said as I walked into At Wick's End seventeen minutes before it officially opened.

Eve said, "Belle and I had a morning routine before the shop opened every morning. We arrive forty-five minutes before the doors are unlocked." She tried to hide the scolding in her voice.

"I had to move my things here from my old apartment," I said, finding it odd that the owner was explaining his nontardiness to his employee like a small child in school. I added, "By the way, if you're interested, I've got a few boxes of Belle's things if you'd like to look through them before I take them to the Salvation Army."

"I do perfectly well on my own," Eve said. The ground we'd made the day before was in danger of slipping away.

"I'm not asking if you want charity," I said, fighting to keep my voice steady. "I thought you might like a keepsake or two, that's all. I'm holding onto a beautiful two-foot candle myself."

Eve's hard edges softened instantly. "The red one? It was the last candle Belle made. Harrison, I'm sorry, I appreciate the offer, I really do." She let out a heavy sigh, then said, "It's not that I resent Belle leaving everything to you, she was perfectly within her rights to do so, but I imagined I'd inherit At Wick's End someday myself." Realizing how it must have sounded, she quickly added, "Not from her death, mind you, but Belle always talked about living at the beach someday, somewhere on the Outer Banks perhaps, and I just naturally assumed, well, we all know what that leads to. Forgive me," she said simply.

I said, "Eve, there's nothing to forgive. You have every right to feel the way you do, but you should know that I want to stay here and keep making candles with you. I can't wait to learn more, and I'm most appreciative you're willing to teach me."

Was that a hint of rose on her cheeks? "That's why I'm here. Would you like to help me get ready for the day? We need to start by pulling stock from the storeroom."

"I'll do it," I said. "I need to learn my way around some-time, and you showed me where everything was yesterday."

"It's just as well you handle that," Eve said. "Belle was very particular about anyone going in the stockroom but her. She knew where everything was all the time, and she didn't want anyone disturbing her system. As a matter of fact, the only time she'd let me step a foot inside was if she needed help. I just wish she'd asked . . ."

As her words faded, I stood there again, not knowing what to do to offer her comfort. Eve took a deep breath, then seemed to calm herself.

Before I could disappear in the back, Eve said, "I noticed you had a visitor last night after hours."

"How in the world could you know that?" I asked.

"Don't worry, I'm no Sherlock Holmes," she said laughing. "There was a puddle near the door, and I noticed a damp towel in the bathroom."

I nodded. "The sheriff came by, and I happened to be down here looking around when the storm hit. He nearly drowned out there."

Was it my imagination, or did Eve's eyes harden for just an instant? "And what did he want with you?"

"He came by to offer his condolences about Belle. I'd been hoping he was following up on the break-in upstairs, but no such luck."

Eve looked surprised by the news. "What are you talk-ing about? What break-in?"

And here I'd thought the tenants at River's Edge were all prescient. "Somebody broke into Belle's place looking for something yesterday. Twice, to be exact. They made a real mess of things."

"What in the world could they have been looking for? Belle didn't keep any money or jewelry around her apart-ment, she didn't believe in owning expensive things. Frankly, I can't imagine anything there worth taking the risk of being caught."

"I have no idea. Don't worry, though, I changed the

locks, so it won't happen again. Did you happen to have a key to Belle's," I asked softly.

"Now why would I have one of those? We worked together, Harrison, but our private lives were just that."

"I didn't mean anything by it," I quickly said. "I just thought she might have left you a spare in case something happened to hers."

"Well she didn't," Eve said abruptly. "Now if you'll excuse me, I've got a great many things to do before we're ready to open."

The storeroom was locked, but I wasn't about to ask Eve about any more keys if I could help it. I walked back to the small cubby of an office that aspired to be a broom closet in another life and started my search. Eve pointedly ignored me as I walked past her. She earnestly scanned the shelves, making notes on a clipboard as she worked. Now what had I said to offend her so? I wasn't looking forward to tiptoeing around my own employee, but at the moment, I needed her a great deal more than she needed me. It appeared I'd have to wear soft-sole shoes for some time to come.

It didn't take long to find the key, as it was hanging on a nail near the entrance. Thank goodness there was a faded tab taped to the key that identified it.

In fact, there were two nails on the wall behind the office door, side by side, and I couldn't help wondering if that was where Belle had kept a spare key to her apartment. It would make it handy for her, and Eve would certainly have known about it. But I'd already asked her about the key, and she'd denied having one. I thought back about precisely what she'd claimed, and suddenly realized that Eve hadn't said a word about having access to a key, just that she hadn't had one in her possession. It was strictly the truth, but missed the implication of it by a mile. Or could I be reading too much in a single naked nail? There could have been a thousand reasons why that nail had been placed there, and I couldn't spend all day guessing. Asking Eve was certainly out of the question, so I had no choice but to drop it. I had enough on my mind as it was.

I had a new trade to learn if I was going to keep Belle's candle shop afloat.

I grabbed the key and unlocked the storeroom door.

A shiver ran through me as I realized that this was where Belle had died just a few days earlier. Why in the world had she been climbing a ladder in the first place, when a strong strapping woman like Eve was nearby? I could reach the top shelf without the stepladder, but I was a good foot taller than Belle had been. She must have had to extend all the way up the small ladder to reach the beeswax sheets and wicks they'd found near her body.

The ladder was leaning against a lower shelf, and I had a sudden urge to break it into a hundred pieces, to burn it or at the very least to throw it away. I went so far as to pick it up, but the touch of the wood turned my stomach, so I put it down where it had been. I backed up against one of the shelves to collect myself and saw something that was otherwise easy to miss. There was a button leaning against one of the boxes, and I noticed the torn threads clinging to it when I picked it up. It was large and brown with an ornate carving on its face, surely one of a kind. I thought about the sweaters I'd packed away upstairs the day before. Had there been anything with similar buttons on it, or could it have been from the clothes Belle had been wearing the night she died?

I found Eve still going over her list. "Does this look familiar? I was wondering if it belonged to Belle."

Eve took the button from me, frowned a moment, then said, "I've been looking all over for this. Where did you find it?"

"In the storeroom," I admitted. "How did you lose it, do you remember?"

Eve said, "Now if I knew that, I'd have looked for it there. My sweater must have caught on one of the shelves when I was helping Belle move something; I lost this weeks ago." She tucked the button in her pocket, then said, "Have you pulled anything from the list I gave you?"

"No, not yet."

"Harrison, we don't have a great deal of time."

"I'll do it now," I said. Did Eve's story make sense? I wondered about it as I pulled items from the list she'd given me. At least the boxes were clearly marked. Surely if a shelf ripped a button off her sweater she would have felt it. Was it possible that Belle hadn't been alone in the storeroom the night she died? Could someone have helped her off that ladder? I couldn't see Eve doing it, but it was possible, I had to admit that much. She had expected to inherit At Wick's End, that much was clear. That started a line of thought I wasn't entirely comfortable with. What if Eve's story was true, that she'd lost the button earlier helping Belle? Did that necessarily rule out the possibility that someone else might have given my great-aunt a shove? It was something I was going to have to consider, no matter how unpleasant the suspicion was. I found a carton of Golden Yellow sheet wax. It was the exact same wax Belle had died trying to retrieve from the top shelf. Eve had said that Belle knew the contents of their storeroom intimately. So why was she looking up there for something that was readily available without the use of a ladder? Was something hidden there, something she didn't want anyone else to see? I pulled every box off the shelf where she'd been reaching, but all they contained were the supplies clearly marked.

Eve knocked on the door before poking her head inside. "Good heavens, Harrison, what are you doing?"

"I was just looking for something."

Eve surveyed the mess. "Well I hope you found it. We're opening in two minutes. Hurry and put what you've got on the shelves out front. You'll just have to clean this up later."

I SPENT THE day trying to work in the candle shop, but I found myself getting in the way more than helping, and Eve was less than patient with me at times. Hanging on her heels and eavesdropping was one of the best ways I had to learn the business, but she was clearly not happy about my constant proximity.

On one of the rare breaks when we didn't have any customers, Eve said, "Harrison, why don't you take a few minutes and clean the storeroom."

"I can take care of that after hours. I want to watch you work."

"Honestly, I can't work with an audience."

I said, "Okay, I'll try to hang back a little more, but how else am I going to learn?"

Eve said, "We have books to teach you all about candlemaking. They'll do a better job than I can."

"How about this? I'll try to stay out of your way. Honest."

She sighed, then asked, "Have you ever run a cash register in any of your previous jobs?"

"I'm a whiz at one," I admitted. "But I want to be able to sell on the floor, and I can't do that until I have a better grounding."

"You need to learn to take small steps before you're ready to tackle selling on the floor. If you run the cash register when things get busy, I'll let you follow me around other times. Is it a deal?"

"I guess so," I said.

She looked at the clock and said, "Why don't you take a quick lunch break?"

"Then I can cover for you?"

She said, "Hardly. I brought my lunch with me. I'll eat here in the store."

I started to protest, but I'd probably pushed her hard enough. It was a fine line, dancing between forcing her to help me and risking running her off entirely. I decided to keep my small advantage and grab a quick bite while things were slow at the shop. I thought about going to The Crocked Pot, but it looked like Millie was really busy with customers. Instead, I jumped into my old truck and drove into town, getting a hot dog and a Coke and driving back to River's Edge as I ate. I knew I wasn't gone long enough from Eve's point of view, but I didn't want to miss a thing.

I bumped into Lucas Young as I walked into the candle shop. "Mr. Young, were you looking for me?"

He nodded. "Eve told me you just went out for lunch."

"I grabbed a quick bite, but I'm back now. What's up?"

"Actually, I was hoping you'd have a bite with me. There are a few other things we need to go over, the sooner the better."

I looked around the store and saw a lone man studying candlemaking kits. Eve overheard the question and said, "Go, Harrison, I have things under control here."

"Are you sure?"

"Absolutely," she said just a little too forcefully.

"Okay, but I won't be gone long."

The lawyer and I walked outside into the beautiful crisp autumn day. I said, "If you'd like, we can find a table at Millie's and I'll keep you company while you eat."

He glanced at his watch, then said, "No, I'm not all that hungry. It was more of an excuse to get out of my office than anything else."

"So you don't have anything for me?"

He patted his briefcase. "I wouldn't say that. Why don't we sit at one of the benches that overlook the river? That way we can have some privacy for our conversation." We found a spot unoccupied in front of the potter's shop and sat down. The attorney reached for his briefcase and said, "I took the liberty of collecting some papers you should see. I'm not sure if you're going to change the system, you certainly can, but Belle hired a team of three of us who work together on small business accounts in the area. I handle the legal issues, one woman does the books and another handles advertising and promotion. At least she did until she moved to California last week. I'm afraid you're on your own in that department."

"I'm not planning on making any changes. To be honest with you, I don't know enough at this point to do anything, but I'm going to learn, you can bet on that."

"That's admirable," he said. "Still, it wouldn't hurt to look over these statements." Young handed me a thick sheaf of papers and said, "If you need help reading these, I'll be glad to offer my assistance."

I looked at the top paper and saw an incredibly high figure. "Is this how much the property's worth?" It was more than I imagined by a factor of ten.

Young laughed sadly. "I'm afraid that's what you owe on the outstanding balance. Your great-aunt had only a minimal down payment, and she hadn't been able to reduce the principal much. Here are your monthly payments."

I nearly choked when I saw the next page. How in the world was I going to come up with that kind of money running a candle shop? "Do the other businesses bring in much in the way of rent?"

"Even at full capacity, you're barely going to be able to make the mortgage payments. And before you think about raising the rents to give yourself some breathing room, your great-aunt locked in such low rates, against my advice, I might add, that it's a stretch to make those payments."

"But Belle managed, didn't she?" The picture was getting gloomier by the minute.

He said, "Initially she had a nest egg to draw from, an emergency fund, if you will."

"Did she leave that account to someone else? You didn't mention that in her assets."

Young ran a hand over his head. "That's because it's all gone. She used it to make up what she owed every month."

I studied the river and thought about jumping in, Young's words were so depressing. He must have sensed the emotions running through me. "Harrison, I know you want to succeed at this, but there's no shame in walking away from this. Even if you could sell the place, I'm not sure how much equity you'd get out of it."

I shook my head. "Belle wanted me to stay, so I'm going to hang on as long as I can."

"That's admirable, but it might not be all that practical."

I said, "I'll make it work. I have to."

The attorney said, "I understand. Listen, if there's anything I can do to help, just let me know. I hate being the bearer of bad news, but I thought you should know what you're up against."

"No, I appreciate the heads-up, I really do."

He said, "Well, I'd better grab a quick bite before my next appointment." He patted me on the shoulder and added, "If you need someone to talk to, I've got a special this month, all the advice you need, free of charge."

I tried to muster a smile, but I knew it was a weak attempt. "Thanks. I might take you up on that."

After he was gone, I found myself wondering just what Belle had gotten me into. If she couldn't make it work, what chance did I have? I'd never held a job more than two years, let alone run a business. I tucked the papers under one arm, promising myself to study them later, then walked back to the candle shop, a great deal of the wind taken out of my sails. It appeared that I was going to have to learn the business even faster than I'd thought.

By the time we were ready to lock the door that night, I was nearly ready to call Mr. Young and have him start the paperwork to sell the place at auction. We had one customer all afternoon, a woman who bought a tea light for half a dollar.

Eve said, "Don't worry, Harrison, our business runs in spells."

"I hope we do better tomorrow," I said, still thinking about that payment hanging over my head without the benefit of Belle's nest egg.

Eve said, "There's not enough to worry about depositing, we'll just leave it for tomorrow. Belle and I did that on occasion."

I said, "Fine. Thanks."

She paused at the door, then said, "Good night, Harrison. I'll see you in the morning."

"Good night."

She added, "Try to get some sleep tonight. You've got a big day tomorrow."

"Let's hope so."

Eve said, "Don't tell me you've forgotten about your

lesson with Mrs. Jorgenson at ten o'clock tomorrow morning. You need to be sharp for that."

"Oh, I remember," I said. After talking with Mr. Young, I knew that now more than ever, it was critical I succeed. I pointed to a stack of books by the register. "I'm taking these upstairs to study tonight."

She walked back to the stack and pulled one out of the pile. "You're just rolling candles tomorrow. Study this one."

I took it from her and locked the door behind her after flipping the OPEN sign to CLOSED. Maybe I could get in a little work before going back upstairs.

No matter how hard I tried, I just couldn't concentrate on what I was reading. After skimming the same page three times, I decided I'd had enough candlemaking for one day, locked up the shop and went upstairs. I nearly tripped over the boxes holding Belle's personal possessions, and I thought about taking them to the Salvation Army, but I didn't have the heart to do it. Getting rid of her things would be almost like turning my back on her. There wasn't much in Belle's refrigerator, but I found some sourdough bread in her freezer and a jar of peanut butter in one of the cabinets. I was going to have to wash it down with water when I found three cans of soda stowed under the counter. It wasn't the most nutritious meal I'd ever had, but I was ashamed to admit that it wasn't the least I'd had either.

After I ate, I decided it was the best time to go through those boxes one last time, and then load them into my truck and get rid of them.

Saving her personal possessions for last, I opened each box of clothing, checked them all one last time, then sorted them into piles. I was surprised to find a crumpled piece of paper in the bottom of one of her pockets. The boldly written note said, "YOU AREN'T GOING TO GET AWAY WITH THIS, I'LL SEE TO THAT." Now what in the world could that be about? It sounded like a threat to me, and I wondered who'd written Belle such a dramatic note. A sudden thought struck me. Could this note be tied to her death? Had the writer carried through with their threat and pushed Belle off that ladder? Something had been going on in my great-aunt's life just before she'd died, and I was starting to get the feeling that her accident hadn't been one after all. I already knew there was no reason for Belle to have been up on that ladder, the boxes of sheet wax on the floor proved that. The note just confirmed my suspicions. How hard would it be to set the scene to make things look like an accident? Belle was older, how old I couldn't imagine, and I could see the police swallowing the setup, no matter how competent Coburn seemed. If he wasn't looking for a homicide, would he see Belle's "accident" for what it was?

I thought about calling him, but I didn't have enough to go on, certainly not enough for his high level of requirement of proof. But there wasn't anything to stop me from looking into Belle's death. I searched the rest of her things for another clue about what might have happened, but there was nothing else that stood out. In the end, I tucked the note in one of Belle's books and tried to get some sleep. Eve was right; tomorrow's lesson with Mrs. Jorgenson might be the deciding factor in whether I could afford to keep running At Wick's End, and I had to be ready for my prize pupil.

THE NEXT MORNING Eve wouldn't even let me out on the sales floor. Instead, I practiced making sheets into candles over and over again. Even at our cost, I wasn't comfortable with how much material I was burning through, but Eve had insisted in the end it would pay off. After a while, I needed a breather, so I went into our office and leafed through the candlemaking book I should have studied the night before. It still couldn't hold my attention though; I was focusing on what might have happened to Belle. The more I thought about it, the more certain I was that someone had stolen the last few years of her life. I was still sitting at the desk thinking about how I was going to prove it when Eve stuck her head into the office after knocking once.

"Mrs. Jorgenson's been waiting out front for five minutes," she said in a hushed whisper, as if announcing the arrival of a pope or a president.

"Why didn't you let me know?" I asked.

"She's been shopping and I've been helping her, but I think she's getting restless. Harrison, you can't keep her waiting," Eve said insistently.

"Then I guess we'd better get started," I said as I closed the book.

I found Mrs. Jorgenson browsing the store shelves, picking up a candle now and then, studying it, then handing it to Eve, who was again waiting by her side with a basket nearly full of candles.

"I trust we're ready to begin," she said in a lordly manner as I walked out into the shop.

"I'm ready if you are," I said as I led her back to the workroom where the classes were held.

Mrs. Jorgenson paused to answer her cell phone, and after a whispered conversation, she offered the caller an exasperated good-bye, shut her telephone off and said, "I'm afraid I've got to reschedule our lesson. Margaret Blaine is in charge of the luncheon at the club, and things are falling apart on her." She looked quite pleased with the news.

With a wave of her hand, Mrs. Jorgenson added, "Still, my visit today was interesting. I found several things I like. I trust we'll be able to begin our lessons tomorrow. Shall we say eleven o'clock?"

"I'll be here," I said, relieved that I'd have more time to prepare, but disappointed that we couldn't get started immediately. I was excited about sharing my newfound knowledge with someone. On second thought, after talking with Mr. Young, I realized I was depending on Mrs. Jorgenson's patronage more than I'd expected.

Mrs. Jorgenson took a few steps toward the door, then stopped and turned back toward me. "Oh my goodness, I just remembered I'm already committed all day tomorrow, I've got a charity board meeting at the hospital. Let's make it Monday. I never go out on the weekends."

To my surprise, I felt like a kid who just found out his midterm tests had been canceled. I was more nervous about teaching than I'd realized.

"Monday will be fine," I said, fighting to keep the joy out of my voice.

Eve rang up Mrs. Jorgenson's purchases, looking at me quizzically a time or two, then handed her the bag. "Thanks for coming by," Eve said as Mrs. Jorgenson left, but the socialite didn't take the trouble to reply.

She was probably already thinking about how she was going to make Margaret Blaine squirm.

If I'd been Margaret, I doubt I would have made the call. Sometimes the frying pan is better than the fire.

Five

BEFORE I could explain to Eve what had happened, a customer came in, one who approached my assistant with a frantic plea for help. As they started to discuss the woman's candlemaking problems, Pearly Gray walked into the store.

"Do you happen to have a moment, Harrison?" he asked with that cultured voice of his.

"I'm all yours. What's up?"

"I just wanted to speak with you about the break-in."

Millie had been right; there was no need for a newsletter for the folks at River's Edge. It appeared the grapevine in place took care of distributing information just fine without it. "I don't know much about it myself," I said. "Mr. Young, Belle's attorney, had just done an inventory of her things, and when he checked the place again, he said nothing was missing."

Pearly frowned. "But then he didn't know your great-aunt as well as some of us did. Who's to say he didn't miss something during his first canvass?"

"Pearly, you haven't always been a handyman, have you?"

"Why do you ask?"

I said, "You just seem a little too . . ."

"Eloquent?" he asked with a smile.

"Exactly."

Pearly paused a moment, then reluctantly admitted, "In another life, I served the world as a clinical psychologist."

"So what happened to bring you here?" One look at his face told me I'd overstepped my bounds. "Sorry, it's really none of my business."

Pearly shook his head. "Actually, I understand your curiosity. Harrison, when I finally realized I couldn't save the world, I decided to lower my sights and keep River's Edge running. It's a glorious old place."

I knew there had to be a lot he wasn't telling me, but I wasn't about to push him any further. I had to get over the fact that Pearly was dressed in a pair of faded bibbed overalls and clunky work boots, and accept the fact that the man was most likely a great deal smarter than I was. It was just so easy to take him at face value based on his appearance and forget the life he'd led before opting to become a handyman.

"If something was stolen from Belle's, it's long gone," I said. "There's nothing anyone can do about it now."

"Still, I'd like to survey the scene on my own, if you don't mind."

Enough was enough. "Pearly, the place has been cleaned up. You're too late to see anything. I've got some boxes ready for the Salvation Army and I've already moved my things upstairs. As far as I'm concerned, the incident's over."

He nodded. "I suppose you're correct. It can be difficult to let go though, can't it?"

I patted his shoulder. "Sometimes that's the only option we have."

I thought the conversation was over, but Pearly hesitated, then added, "By the way, the new lock was an excellent idea."

"Thanks. I get them every now and then," I said, then added a smile so he could see I was joking. Before Pearly could leave, I asked, "Since I've got you here, I'd like to ask you something. What do you know about this Markum fellow upstairs?"

"The salvage and recovery gent? Truthfully, we haven't had the opportunity to get to know one another yet. He keeps pretty well to himself, and from what I've seen, his office hours are only at night. Belle joked that he must be some kind of vampire to work when he does. Well, I'd better scat. Aaron Gaston has a leak in his sink, and potters are absolutely anal about their water supply. Have you met Aaron yet?"

"No, is he the one who runs The Pot Shot?"

"He's the man. An unusual fellow, not somebody you'd pick out of the crowd as an artist, but the gentleman is a true talent. He's been teaching me pottery, or at least attempting to. You should take lessons yourself, if you're interested, they're quite reasonable. Fascinating hobby, pottery. The clay has a mind of its own sometimes. Now if you'll excuse me, I'd better get to that sink."

After Pearly was gone, I found myself wondering how he'd known I'd had the lock replaced upstairs. Was he being a good handyman, prepared to offer to replace it himself when he spotted the new work, or had he tried to gain reentry to continue his search and been foiled by the replacement? His offer to look around Belle's place could have been a friendly gesture, or it could mean Pearly wasn't ready to give up his search. I was learning one thing—investigating Belle's death was making me suspicious of everyone in her life. It was amazing how many things could be twisted when I started with that frame of reference.

MY STOMACH WAS just starting to growl from hunger when Heather from The New Age came in with a picnic basket. "Harrison, how would you like to join me for lunch?"

"That sounds great. Let me check with Eve first, though, and make sure she doesn't need me here."

After Eve assured me that I could take all the time I needed, a little too enthusiastically for my taste, I joined Heather at the door of At Wick's End.

"Does this mean you're free?" she asked.

"I got the distinct impression I'm not exactly crucial to At Wick's End's operation at the moment."

Heather laughed. "Oh, pooh, you're just learning, Harrison. These things take time."

Outside, the autumn day was glorious, the sunshine warm enough to enjoy but without the brutal heat and intensity of summer. Though we were near the mountains, we still got blistering summer temperatures nearly as much as Charlotte and Hickory did. No doubt about it, autumn was my favorite time of year. I loved to see the changing leaves decorate the world with their pallets of color and taste the air scrubbed clean and fresh, with just a hint of the chill to come.

I took in a deep breath, then asked Heather, "So where should we eat?"

"If you don't mind the concrete steps, I nearly always eat my lunch near the river. You can't imagine the things you see float by."

"That sounds good," I said as I followed her down the steps that led to the water.

After we found a spot we liked, Heather opened her basket and pulled out sandwiches carefully wrapped in brown paper. I took one offered and said, "I'm starving. What are we eating?"

She held her wrapped sandwich up and said, "I made us bean sprouts. They're really great."

I tried to hide my disappointment. What else should I have expected from a hippie shop owner? I should have realized that a club sandwich would be out of the question before I agreed to come.

Trying to put the best face on things, I promised myself

I'd choke it down if I could and never accept another invitation without knowing what was on the menu first.

I unwrapped the sandwich with no great haste. "Hey, it's ham on rye."

Heather grinned impishly. "Dijon mustard too. You should have seen your face when I told you it was bean sprouts. What would you like to drink? I've got Dr Pepper and Mountain Dew."

I took the Dr Pepper and twisted the top off the iced bottle. After taking a healthy swallow, I said, "Okay, I admit that I might have misread you."

Heather smiled brightly. "Then I'll confess to setting you up just then. I love bean sprouts, but I wasn't about to force my tastes on you, especially not during our first shared meal. So what do you think of River's Edge so far?"

I took a bite of my sandwich as I considered the question. "It's quite a collection, isn't it?"

"Of businesses or people?" she asked.

"To be honest with you, both."

Heather nodded. "That's why I love it so much. Not many nine-to-five types here, unless you count Gary Cragg, and he's an oddity in his own way."

"What do you mean?" I asked.

She said, "My experience has been that most lawyers cluster together near the courthouse. I've often wondered what he's doing out here by himself." She took a bite from her sandwich, then added, "If I'm being honest about it, it could just be the suit I've got problems with. I've never been all that impressed with anybody who has to wear a tie to work. I doubt Gary has ever been on a picnic in his life."

I smiled softly. "Maybe you should have invited him instead of me."

Heather shook her head. "I don't think so, Harrison. I made the right choice."

I nodded my thanks. "I'm honored you asked."

A pair of mallard ducks swam by us near the shore,

pausing now and then to dive for something in the water. Heather tossed a piece of her bread to them, and they attacked it with zeal. I followed suit with the little that remained of my sandwich, popping the last of the meat in my mouth as I threw the bread. They waited around another minute after gobbling it down just as quickly, realized the lunch counter was closed, then went back to their fishing.

"It's really peaceful here, isn't it," I said, mesmerized by the drifting currents of the water.

"It can be," she replied. "Hey, did you ever get rid of those boxes for the Salvation Army?"

"Not yet. I've been so busy around the store, I haven't had a chance."

Heather put the last of the wrappings in her basket as she said, "The offer's still open if you need me to drop them off for you."

"Thanks, I'll keep that in mind," I said as I stood and stretched. The concrete had been a hard seat, but I hadn't realized how hard until I stood up. I dusted off my hands and said, "I'll have to return the favor sometime soon. Thanks again for lunch," I said as I walked back to At Wick's End.

"You're most welcome," she said. "I'm here every day at noon. Just let me know."

After I was back inside the candle shop, I couldn't help wondering if Heather's lunch invitation had been just another way to get a crack at those boxes again, or if it was, as it appeared, a friendly gesture welcoming me to the building. I told myself, "Harrison, old boy, you're going to have to stop seeing villainous motives behind every action, or you'll drive yourself crazy."

But how was I going to recognize something that really was a clue, if I didn't examine every action and motive I ran across?

Detective work surely wasn't as easy as they made it look in books.

* * *

I FOUND EVE in the office having a sandwich of her own. "Sorry, I didn't know you were eating," I said as I started to back out of the room.

She patted the chair across from her. "Sit, keep me company. Belle and I always used to split our lunch breaks, but if no one was in the shop, we'd share a bite or two together."

I sat where she directed. "You must really miss her."

Eve nodded. "It's amazing how large a hole somebody can leave in your life when they're gone." She stared at the remains of her sandwich, took another bite, then said, "It's just not ever going to be the same around here."

"You know, you're free to go somewhere else if you'd like if it's too painful," I said gently. I could see that I'd worded it badly by the way she reacted, but before she could say a word of retort, I added, "Not that I don't appreciate you staying on. Eve, I'm the first person to admit that I don't know how I'd run the shop without you. But it sounds like losing Belle might be more than you can take and stay on here at the shop."

Eve tossed the unfinished bite of her sandwich in her bag, then threw the whole thing into the trash. "I'm staying," she said firmly.

"Because you want to?" I asked gently.

"Because I have to," Eve blurted out. "I love candles. Where else am I going to be able to find someone to pay me to be around them all day? I'll go if you want me to, Harrison, but it won't be willingly. You might need a little help throwing me out."

"Eve, you've got your job as long as you want it," I said. Now why did I say that? If she turned out to be the one who had shoved Belle off that ladder, she'd be gone as fast as I could turn her over to the police. But until I knew without a doubt that she'd been the one, I needed Eve's presence at Wick's End more than she needed me.

"I'm glad that's settled," Eve said as she brushed at a few nonexistent crumbs on the desktop. "Now let's get to work and teach you how to pour candles. It's the next logical step in your training."

UNFORTUNATELY, IT WAS not to be. We had a steady stream of customers the rest of the afternoon, something Eve told me was rare enough to savor. As before, I worked the register while she helped our clientele, and by the time we put our CLOSED sign up, I was beat from standing on my feet all afternoon. That was one good thing, probably the only good thing, about selling those computers; most of the time I could do it sitting down behind my desk.

As I turned the lock and pulled down the door shade, I said, "Man, I'm beat."

Eve said, "You can't stop now, Harrison. There's more work that needs to be done before we're ready to go home."

I smiled softly. "Point me in the right direction and I'll get to it."

"We need to restock the shelves, total the day's receipts, then you need to take our deposit by the bank. I've done it when I've had to, but carrying cash around town makes me nervous."

It suddenly hit me that I knew nothing about the ins and outs of running the place myself. "I don't even know how much money you make. When do you get paid? Do I cut you a check myself or should I pay you in cash out of the register?"

Eve smiled. "Relax, Harrison, Belle had a system in place before we opened our doors. Ann Marie Hart does our bookkeeping. She's the one who cuts my check, yours too if you keep Belle's system in place. Instead of taking money off the top, Belle drew a salary just like I do, then she gave us both Christmas bonuses every year."

"That sounds like a good plan," I said.

Eve added, "When we had good years, it worked out quite nicely. Some of my bonuses at first were in the form of supplies when she couldn't afford to give me cash."

I nodded. "It sounds like I need to talk to Ann Marie."

Eve creased her lips, and I asked, "Did I say something wrong?"

"No, but I may have jumped the gun. I've already set up an appointment for you with her first thing Monday morning. Don't worry, you'll be finished before Mrs. Jorgenson gets here, Ann Marie's an early riser, and she doesn't dawdle or waste time if she doesn't have to."

"That works for me, but until then, what do I do with our deposit tonight?"

"I'll show you how to balance our receipts with the register tape," she said. "Ninety-nine times out of a hundred, they match perfectly."

"And if they don't?"

"Then we order something from Millie and stay here until they do."

Amazing as it was given the fact that I'd run the register most of the day, we balanced out to the penny. After a quick lesson at logging the deposit and filling out the slip, Eve said, "Now you're ready to deposit this at the bank."

"Let me grab my truck keys," I said, "and I'll take it right now."

"Why don't you take Belle's truck? It's yours now too."

That certainly got my attention. "Are you telling me my great-aunt had a truck?"

Eve said, "In this business, you need one, believe me. We do more than just the shop, Harrison. There are street fairs, demonstrations, all sorts of times where you'll be on the road representing At Wick's End. Mr. Young should have mentioned it to you."

"Where is this mystery truck?" I asked.

"Behind the building parked in Belle's spot. I guess that's yours too now."

I pocketed the keys to my old Dodge Ram, a pickup truck on its last legs, and followed Eve outside, the zippered deposit bag tucked under my arm. There was a two-tone brown Ford pickup with a brown camper top over the long bed parked in back of the store. "Wow, she's a beauty," I said the second I saw it.

"It's nearly ten years old, but Belle babied it," Eve said as she handed me the keys. "Don't forget, we bank with Micah's Ridge Community Bank. None of those big corporate conglomerates for Belle. She believed in doing business with local folks whenever she could manage it."

I nodded absently and unlocked the truck. There were running boards on the side, no doubt to help Belle step up into the cab. This was a luxury addition, with carpeting, automatic transmission, cruise control and even four-wheel drive. "Unbelievable. Belle was just full of surprises, wasn't she?"

"More than you'll ever know," Eve said.

I started the engine, then said, "Can I drop you off anywhere?"

"No thank you. I walk whenever I can, and ride when I have to. Have a good evening, Harrison. I'll see you in the morning." As she started away, she stopped and turned back. "You did a fine job today."

Before I could reply, she was gone.

I dropped the deposit off at the bank without any problems, and thought about taking the truck out for a spin, but ultimately decided I needed to get back to River's Edge. I was discovering that having property involved more than just collecting the rent. It was more like being the mayor of a small town. Owning River's Edge must have been perfect for Belle. Never the type to complain about being lonely, nonetheless I was sure that the varied group of tenants occupying space there was all the immediate family she really needed around her.

The one thing that kept recurring as I talked with the folks who knew my great-aunt best, day in and day out, was her warm heart.

I'd really missed out by not making her more of a part

of my life than I did. And now the opportunity was gone forever.

I'd do the next best thing though. I'd do my best to carry on the legacy she'd given me. And if I could manage it, I'd find the person who'd taken her from us all too soon.

Six

I found a note from Gary Cragg taped to my apartment door when I got back from the bank. In hastily written cursive, *Don't forget our appointment* was scrawled on the back of his business card. So much for my plans to take a long hot shower and read a little to unwind from a full day at the shop. I looked longingly at my apartment door, then walked to the attorney's office down the hall.

Cragg was at his desk working through a stack of papers when I knocked on the doorjamb.

"If you're tied up, we can talk another time," I said, hoping for a reprieve from our meeting.

"Nonsense, I'll just be a moment," he said as he finished proofreading a document, clearly a letter, before signing it in a flourish of script that was fancier than I would have ever expected from him.

He started to pick up another letter and I stood up. "Listen, I don't have all night. We can talk some other time."

Cragg reluctantly put the letter down and said, "Stay. This can wait." He leaned back in his leather chair and said, "Harrison, I know inheriting this white elephant from your aunt was more than you bargained for."

"She was my great-aunt, and yes, I was surprised when I found out she'd left all of River's Edge to me."

Cragg nodded. "Exactly. Now this establishment was a fine match for Mrs. Black, but you're a relatively young man with his life still ahead of him. You surely don't want to be burdened by the arduous task of running this building. The tenants are, as kindly as I can put it, all rather eccentric. Therefore," he said as he leaned forward and held up a document from his desktop, "I'm willing to offer you a considerable sum to alleviate all of your problems immediately. Sign this, and you'll have more money than you would have cleared in five years selling those second-rate computers you've been peddling."

"But this place is mortgaged to the hilt," I blurted out.

"Once the property is in my possession, I have no doubts that I will be able to turn a reasonable profit above what I'm willing to pay you. Given your recent salary history, it's a quite generous offer."

So the attorney had done his homework about my past work. Not only did he know where I'd worked, but most likely he'd discovered the dismal amount of pay I was used to. I took the document from him, studied the figure on the paper, then frowned at it in surprise. I had no idea how much River's Edge was truly worth above and beyond what I owed the bank, but I doubted it was possible it was worth that much. It didn't really matter. Mr. Young had made it quite clear why I couldn't sell the place before I'd been there five years, but I wasn't ready to admit that, at least not until I had a chance to see just how badly Cragg wanted it, and why.

"You know, now that I think about it, this figure seems a little low," I said as I floated the paper back across the desk to him. It was all I could do to keep from grinning as I said it. I would have said the same thing no matter how much he'd offered. I was looking for a great deal more than a higher price on a parcel I was in no position to sell.

Cragg looked at me a moment, tore up the document, and to my surprise, the man actually smiled as he handed me another piece of paper. "It appears you are more savvy than I credited you for. This figure should be more to your liking."

I studied the substantially higher number for a few moments. Cragg was serious about acquiring River's Edge, if that second offer meant anything. I still didn't know why though.

I said, "I'm sorry, I shouldn't have let this go on as long as I have. River's Edge is not for sale."

"Mr. Black, let me assure you, the offer in your hands is well above the current market value of the property. No one is going to be willing to match it, let alone top it."

"I'm not disputing that," I said. "Just out of curiosity, why are you willing to pay more than you admit it's worth? I'm not about to believe it's for the place's sentimental value."

Cragg stroked his desk lightly. "You're wrong, there, I have grown quite fond of River's Edge." He shook his head, then added, "However, you are correct in the assumption that there is more driving me than emotion. I plan to evict the other tenants and turn this entire building into a legal complex. We're close enough to the courthouse to walk, and once the papers are signed, I'm certain I can persuade several of my colleagues to join me."

I slid the second paper back to him as well. "It's a moot point, actually. I couldn't sell you River's Edge even if I wanted to. Belle added a clause to her will that forbids me from selling the complex, at least any time soon."

Cragg smiled without warmth. "Believe me, we can break that proviso without any problem. All I need is your approval, and I can move immediately."

I stood. "Even if you're right, I'm not willing to part with River's Edge. I'm more interested in Belle's intent than I am in breaking her last request."

"Your decision is final then?" he asked, the hard edge coming out in his voice.

"My hands are tied," I said. "If not entirely by the law, then by my great-aunt's desires, and those are more important to me than any document."

Without another word, Cragg destroyed the paper I'd returned to him, then he turned his attention back to the stack of papers on his desk. I was as effectively dismissed as I had ever been in my entire life.

It appeared that one of my tenants was already unhappy with his new landlord.

That was just too bad for him. I never was one to respond well to pressure.

When somebody pushes me, I have a tendency to push back.

I HAD TO walk past Markum's mysteriously vague salvage-and-recovery operation to get back to my apartment. I was dog-tired, but my curiosity outweighed my desire for that hot shower.

I knocked on the door, waited thirty seconds, then knocked again, this time quite a bit harder than before.

No reply. Jiggling the handle, I discovered that the door was locked. It appeared that Markum was not in.

So what was the sound of voices I heard coming from the other side of the door? I patted my pockets and came up with an old grocery list and scratched out a quick note on the back of it. *Would like to meet you. Harrison Black, Belle's place.*

After sliding it under the door, I headed back to my new apartment. It was time for that shower after all.

GLORY BE, HOT water was not a problem in my new accommodations. I don't know how long I stood under the pounding heat of the shower, but by the time I shut the water off, my fingers were starting to prune up. As I walked into the kitchen, toweling my hair dry, I lit Belle's candle, most likely the last one she'd ever made, and

watched as the wick jumped to life. The flame, strong and
steady, reminded me of Belle, a solid part of my early life.
There was a hint of cinnamon in the air that I loved. It
reminded me again of sweet rolls, apple pie and the Snickerdoodle cookies. I let the candle burn as I cooked myself a
pasta dinner, and kept it glowing while I ate. At the rate it
was burning, I'd have that candle memorial for a month, a
fitting period of mourning for my great-aunt.

Later, after the dishes were done, I went prowling
around the apartment for something to read. Belle was an
avid reader. She'd been the one who'd gotten me hooked
on the printed word, mysteries in particular, giving me a
complete set of Agatha Christies on my ninth birthday.
Okay, I'd asked for a new baseball glove, but by the time
I'd read *The Mysterious Affair at Styles,* I was lost forever.
I've never been without a book to read since, though my
past living conditions made it tough to keep them after I'd
read them.

Belle had an extensive collection of books on hand,
and I'd had to force myself not to start browsing as I'd
reshelved them from their tumbles to the floor. Amaz-
ingly enough, none of them had been damaged in their
short falls. There was her own complete set of Agatha
Christie books present, though hers were hardcovers
instead of the paperbacks she'd given me. Judging from
the number and variety of titles on the shelves, she'd kept
her interest in mysteries through the years, with books
from the latest bestseller lists mingling with classics from
the Golden Age of mystery. I chose one of the Agatha
Christies at random, curled up on the couch, and quickly
found myself revisiting a world full of English villages,
vicars and tea.

It nearly jarred me off the couch when the telephone
rang.

"Hello," I said, marking my place with one finger,
unwilling to put the book down.

"So it's true," I heard a familiar feminine voice say on

the other end of the line. "You've moved out of your apartment after all."

"Hi, Becka. I'm surprised to hear from you. How'd you find me?" Becka Lane and I had dated off and on for the past few years, but three months ago she'd decided we were finished for good. She had declared with more frustration than regret that I'd never amount to anything, and she was tired of waiting for me to make something of my life. I'd been more relieved than heartbroken with her declaration, a sign that told me we were probably both just waiting for the other one to give up first.

She said, "It was the oddest thing, Harrison. I was out running around today and I went by your place. I don't know what hit me, but I suddenly wanted to see you again. I can't tell you how stunned I was to find you'd moved."

I knew without a doubt how she'd gotten my new number. I was sure Mrs. Harper had been delighted to share the information. She'd always wanted the two of us to get together. "There was nothing there for me anymore," I said.

There was a pause, then Becka said, "Aren't you going to invite me over to your new place? I'm dying to see it, and my schedule's completely open."

"Sorry, but I'm not in any shape for company tonight," I said.

Most likely it was a first for Becka, being turned down like that. "Come on, Harrison, I won't stay long. I'd just really like to see you tonight."

"You're welcome to come by the shop sometime," I said, knowing that Mrs. Harper had no doubt shared that particular news with her as well.

"Absolutely, I have every intention of coming by, but I thought we could get together tonight. I've got some of your favorite wine," she added, ignoring my refusal completely.

It was time to be blunt. "Listen, I'm beat. I'm going to bed." I didn't even give her a chance to protest as I hung up the telephone. It appeared that Becka had forgotten how nasty she'd been while breaking up with me, but the "I never want to see you again" still rang in my ears.

In another minute, I was back in Dame Agatha's world, happy to leave mine far behind.

A POUNDING ON the apartment door brought me fully awake. I'd dozed off on the couch reading, and looked at the nearest clock through blurred vision.

It was 2:00 AM.

Whoever wanted to get in was quite adamant about it.

I picked up an old baseball bat I'd found cleaning out Belle's closet, something she'd probably kept for self-defense herself.

"Who is it," I called out through the door, studying the man on the other side through the peephole. He was huge, with shoulders that would barely fit through the doorway. His hair was the color of midnight, untamed and wild.

"It's Markum. I got your note."

I opened the door, the bat still firmly clutched in one hand. "It's two o'clock in the morning," I protested. Close up, the man had the greenest eyes I'd ever seen, as if they had been cut from the coldest emeralds on earth.

Markum shrugged. "Sorry, I was on the telephone when you came by earlier. Long distance, different time zones, that sort of thing. What can I do for you?"

I dropped the bat on the couch as I walked deeper into the apartment, Markum close behind me. "I just thought it would be nice to meet you, since I've just inherited the building."

"Sorry about your great-aunt," he said easily. "You don't happen to have any coffee around, do you?"

"I've got instant," I said, going for my transported stash in the freezer.

"No, I'd rather go without than drink that slag," he said with a grimace. "If that's it, I'll be going then."

"Excuse my asking, but I was wondering what exactly it

is you salvage and recover," I asked, the lateness of the hour accounting for my direct approach.

He grinned slightly. "Oh, this and that. If it's gone, I've got a knack for finding it."

"And I bet you go here and there to do it, don't you?" I replied.

"Now you've got it. If that's it, I'm going to go scrounge up some real java."

"Thanks for stopping by," I said.

He nodded and headed out the door. What an odd bird he was. I'd learned absolutely nothing about him, except for the fact that if he'd wanted Belle dead, shoving her off that ladder wouldn't have been a problem for him at all.

Now that I was wide awake, what in the world was I going to do with myself for the next six hours? Going back to sleep was out of the question; once I'm up, I'm up. It was a curse I'd had since childhood.

There was really only one thing I could do that made any sense at all. I got dressed quickly and headed down to At Wick's End.

"YOU'RE HERE EARLY," Eve said as she came in, removing her jacket and hanging it carefully up on a peg in the office.

"I couldn't sleep," I said, "So I thought I'd get some work done."

Eve looked worriedly around. "I hope you haven't switched anything around. Belle and I worked out the perfect system for our inventory, and I'd hate to see it . . . modified."

I shook my head. "I didn't change a thing. Actually, I've been studying." I gestured to the eclectic collection of candlemaking books lying open in front of me.

She caught me yawning and said, "Harrison, your work here is important, but you certainly didn't need to lose any sleep over it."

I considered telling her about my late-night caller and

my inability to get back to sleep, but decided to let her think I'd been up cramming for my new career. I gestured to one of the open books in front of me. "It's all quite fascinating, isn't it?"

"It certainly can be," Eve said. "So, should we get started on that pouring lesson before the brunt of our Saturday crafters come in?"

"Is Saturday a big day for the store?" I asked.

"Normally it's our biggest," she admitted. "Shall we stick to our system yesterday? You did quite well on the register."

"I should be fine as long as the prices are marked."

"They should be, but don't hesitate to ask. Now let's go get some supplies so we can get a quick lesson in before the rush begins."

UNFORTUNATELY, THAT LESSON was going to have to wait. Before we could even collect our supplies, customers started flowing in at an amazing rate.

There was barely time to eat our lunches in hurried ten-minute shifts, and by the time we were five minutes from locking the door that evening, I was exhausted.

"Why don't we go ahead and lock up early?" I suggested.

Eve said, "Harrison, it's your store to do with as you wish, but Belle always believed that if the hours were posted, they should be honored."

"Okay, I understand that." I started straightening up the sales counter and added, "Thanks, Eve."

"Selling candles is what I do, Harrison."

I said, "No, I didn't mean that. Well, I do, but what I'm really thanking you for is staying on and helping me run this place."

"I didn't have much choice, Belle would haunt me for the rest of my life if I deserted you in your time of need." She patted my hand gently. "I believe we'll make a candle-maker out of you yet." She checked her watch and said, "Two minutes till closing. It's been a good day."

The warmth of her words didn't last nearly long enough when I heard a familiar voice coming from the front.

"Is anybody here?"

It looked like Becka was following through with her threat to visit me at Wick's End. I'd forgotten all about her promised visit, but apparently she'd meant it when she'd threatened to drop by.

Seven

"I'LL take care of her," Eve said as I finished neatening the display of tea lights on the counter.

"I wish you could," I said.

"Pardon me?"

"It's an old acquaintance of mine," I admitted. "And she's not here to shop for candles."

"I understand," Eve said, though clearly she didn't. Heck, I didn't get it myself. Why was Becka suddenly trying to get back into my life? The breakup had been final, at least from her end of things. I'd managed to get over her without too much of a problem, though I'd only dated a few times since we'd split. One thing was certain—I knew better than anyone else that it was time to move forward and not back. The last thing I needed in my life at that moment was a walk down that particular memory lane.

Becka rushed to embrace me when I walked toward her, but she must have gotten the hint when I didn't return her enthusiasm.

"Going somewhere special this evening," I asked as I took in her carefully coiffed blond hair, her stylish outfit with a short skirt sure to raise more than a few eyebrows of our conservative clientele, and enough Obsession to drown out the strongest scented candle we had in stock.

"I came to see you, Harrison. Surely that's enough of a reason to get dressed up, isn't it?"

"I'll have to take your word for it. I guess you're here for your tour of the shop, but we're just about ready to close up for the day. In all honesty, I didn't know you were that interested in candles."

Becka frowned. "Harrison, if you had inherited an art gallery or a restaurant, I'd be just as interested in that."

I nodded, suspecting as much. "So whatever windfall I managed to come into, you'd be more than willing to jump back into my life. I understand, it all makes perfect sense now."

Becka frowned gently at me. "Harrison, are you trying to be difficult?"

I grinned. "No, but sometimes it just comes naturally. I'd love to stay and chat, Becka, but I'm kind of busy at the moment. Thanks for stopping by, though."

I saw Eve frowning from the back of the candle shop, and knew I was setting myself up for another lecture on customer service, but this was one customer I was just as glad not to have shopping at Wick's End.

Becka looked around the empty store and said, "Yes, I can see you're up to your eyebrows in customers at the moment."

"As I said, we're closing."

She moved closer to me, nearly knocking me over with her perfume. I never should have told her I liked that particular scent, not if there was a chance she was going to suffocate me with it.

In a voice nearly a whisper, she said, "I admit it, I was too hard on you when we broke it off. I'm sorry, Harrison." When she saw her apology wasn't having the desired effect, she added, "What do I have to do here, get down on my knees and beg?"

"No, I'd hate to see you ruin a new pair of hose," I said.

"Becka, I'm starting a new life here. I don't mean to be ugly about it, but I'm not interested in repeating old mistakes with you. You were right to break up with me, I should have had the guts to do it myself, so let's just leave it at that, shall we? I'm excited about this opportunity, and I'm not just talking about the store. I figure that's the real gift my great-aunt wanted me to have."

She pursed her lips, then said, "I'm not giving up on you, Harrison. I'll be back."

Before I had the chance to reply, she was gone.

Eve came out, so I decided to fire a preemptive strike before her lecture started. "Okay, I was a little rough on her, but Becka's no customer, she's an old girlfriend."

"That's not it," Eve said, a puzzled look on her face as she stared out the door after Becka. "That young lady looks familiar to me for some reason."

"I can't imagine anyone ever seeing Becka and forgetting her," I said. "She's got a way of being noticed that's tough to hide."

Eve said, "Something's different about her, but I swear I'd recognize her anywhere." Suddenly, she said, "I've got it. She's been here before."

"Eve, I can't imagine Becka coming into At Wick's End, not without admitting it to me."

She said adamantly, "The young lady had a scarf around her hair, and her attire was quite a bit more conservative, but I saw her here. I know it."

"So she came in candle shopping one day," I said. "There aren't that many choices in Micah's Ridge."

"You don't understand, Harrison. The real reason I remember her is because she was fighting with Belle about something when I walked in, and the next thing I knew that girl was storming out of here as if she were on fire."

"When did this happen?" I asked, chilled by the thought of Becka fighting with my great-aunt Belle.

"Two days before Belle died," Eve said simply.

* * *

AS MUCH AS I hated the idea, I was going to have to speak with Becka again and find out if Eve's declaration was true. What could Becka have been fighting with Belle about? How did she even discover we were related? I didn't remember telling them about each other. My private life was just that, and I'd never introduced any of my girlfriends to my great-aunt. Truth be told, none of them were all that permanent.

Still, I had to dig deeper and see if it was possible that Becka could have had anything to do with my great-aunt's death.

A headache that had been hovering just out of range suddenly slammed down on me, pounding so hard I could barely see.

Eve was right; Saturday was hopping at Wick's End. I knew we'd sold a lot of supplies over the course of the day, but the total surprised me as I went over the deposit after we finally locked up for the night. I've never been that big a fan of cash, but clearly I was in the minority, at least when it came to our customers. Not that there weren't plenty of checks and credit card receipts in the bundle too, but the tens and twenties were in abundant supply.

After the front shades were pulled, I said, "That was some rush. Is it always this crazy?"

"Not a chance, Harrison. I think every regular customer we ever had came by today."

"To pay their respects?" I asked, stunned by the outpouring for Belle from her customers.

Eve shrugged. "Most of them were sincere, I'm sure, but I'm willing to wager a lot of them were coming by to see if we were CTD."

"What's that mean?"

Eve explained with a slight blush, "CTD stands for 'circling the drain'. One of our best customers works in the Emergency Room over at County Hospital. I suppose I picked up the lingo from her."

"They think we're going under?"

"It's not that outlandish a thought, Harrison. When word

traveled through the crafting circles that a neophyte inherited At Wick's End, what else could they think?"

I threw the deposit into the bag and said, "They could think we're going to be just fine. What do you think, Eve?"

The question obviously startled her for a moment, so I added, "I want your brutally honest opinion."

"That's all I ever give," she said with a wry smile. Eve pondered the question a few moments, then said, "Honestly? Belle kept the store afloat, but she wasn't much on promotions and advertising. If things stay the way they were, we'll do well to break even."

I'd been told by too many people how borderline the operation was. "Breaking even isn't going to be good enough. I know how you feel about the tradition of the place, but I want this shop to succeed. If that means we have to try new things in order to bring in more customers, so be it."

"What did you have in mind?"

I tucked the zippered bag with our deposits under one arm as I headed for the door. "Give me a few days until I can polish my ideas, then we'll talk about them." That was purely smoke and mirrors. I didn't have a clue yet what I was going to do, but by Monday night I would.

After thirty minutes at the library, I had accumulated enough articles on running a small business to take me a month to digest. I gathered up my copies and headed back to the truck. After I dropped the bank deposit off, I planned to dig a little deeper into some of the sheets I'd printed out.

When I got to the parking lot, I walked toward Belle's truck and saw that someone had broken the passenger window.

My heart raced as I hurried to the vehicle, but my worst fears were realized when I saw the empty deposit bag on the floor of the cab—the one that had just recently been brimming with cash. The checks and credit card receipts were scattered in a mess on the floor, but all of the cash was gone.

How in the world was I going to explain to Eve that I'd

forgotten to do the deposit before I went to the library, and had ended up losing so much of our hard-earned money?

THANKFULLY, EVE WAS gone by the time I got back to the store. I had two options: call her at home and ruin her weekend, or wait until tomorrow.

Okay, I never said I was the bravest soul in the world. The bad news could wait.

I tore up the deposit slip, subtracted the healthy cash amount from the total and drove that truck straight to the bank, not even stopping to have the glass fixed along the way. That's what I should have done in the first place. How simple it seemed in hindsight, to take care of business first and save my research for later. I'd learned a valuable, though rather costly lesson, one I swore I'd always remember.

I'D FORGOTTEN ALL about eating, I'd been so upset by the theft I'd invited by leaving the deposit unattended and in plain sight. Millie found me on the steps of the river as she locked up The Crocked Pot. I had no idea how long I'd been sitting there, watching the current flow past in its relentless journey south.

"Hungry?" she asked, shaking a bag at me.

"Not really," I said as my stomach rumbled, proving me a liar.

She sat beside me on the step and forced the bag on me. "I saw you moping out here like you'd just lost your last friend. What troubles can you have that a sandwich can't fix?"

I shook my head, then told her about my incredible lapse in judgment.

I half-expected her to rebuke me, but instead I found understanding in Millie's gaze. "Harrison, you're entitled to a few boneheaded mistakes at the beginning. That's part and parcel of running your own business. You want to hear my biggest blunder?"

"I can't imagine you doing anything as bad as I did."

She laughed heartily, and I found myself smiling despite my gloom. "Don't bet the farm on it, my friend. I was catering a big affair for the mayor the first week I opened. I had four turkeys in my ovens, all the extras made ahead of time, a waitstaff hired, everything in its place. I had a thousand things to do, and when I came back into the kitchen to check on the birds for the first basting a few hours later, I didn't smell a thing. That's when I realized that though I'd set the temperatures on every oven, I'd neglected to turn any of them on."

I chuckled gently. "That's terrible. What did you do?"

"I ran by the grocery store, wiped out their deli and lost my shirt on the deal. I couldn't even salvage the turkeys, they'd been sitting out uncooked too long. Things are bound to happen, Harrison."

"How am I going to face Eve?"

Millie said, "She's a wonderful employee, and you're lucky to have her, but remember, she works for you, Harrison. Nobody's going to lose financially from your mistake but you. That's another thing about running a business. The buck starts and stops with you. That includes the good, the bad and everything in between." She stood, and I joined her.

"Thanks, Millie, you've helped a lot."

"All part of being a friend, Harrison. Now if you'll excuse me, George is taking me out for dinner tonight, and I'd better get home and change."

"Where can he possibly take a woman who cooks as wonderfully as you do?"

Millie smiled. "We're going to a pig picking. I can barbecue pork if I have to, but it's a real luxury to have someone else cook for me. Care to join us? Lots of eligible gals will be around, you can bet on that."

"I'm not in the mood or the market just now," I said. "I've got my hands full with At Wick's End."

"There's always time for a little romance," Millie said, the twinkle nearly blinding in her eyes.

Heather walked out of her shop and saw us standing there. "Hey you two, what's up?"

Millie raised an eyebrow at me, one Heather couldn't see, and said, "I was just leaving, but you could keep Harrison company if you've a mind to." She got up and looked back at me and said, "Don't forget, Harrison, there's always time for that."

Heather said, "What was that all about?"

"Millie was just cheering me up." I wasn't about to go into my story again. Much of the sting was gone, salved by Millie's soft words. Besides, I didn't want everyone at River's Edge to know what a knucklehead I'd been.

"Yeah, I saw your truck window out back. You need to get some cardboard in that if you can't get it fixed right away. It's supposed to rain tonight."

I suddenly realized Heather's storeroom had a window that looked out onto the parking lot in back of River's Edge. Some of the grapevine started to make more sense once I got a better lay of the land.

"I'll do that," I said. Suddenly I realized I wasn't all that crazy about being alone. "Listen, I can't afford anything fancy, but I was wondering if you'd like to catch a bite with me tonight. Unless you already have plans," I added. "I know it's short notice, being Saturday night and all."

Heather said, "I don't have a plan in the world. I was just going to get a pizza and chill out."

"That sounds great," I said. "Do you know any good places around here?"

"Have you ever been to A Slice of Heaven?"

"I've never heard of it," I admitted.

"Harrison, you are in for a real treat. Why don't I drive, though. There's no glass on my seats."

I said, "We can take my other truck, if you'd like."

"The Dodge?" she asked. "No thanks, but I might want to borrow it sometime. Now there's a truck bed I wouldn't feel guilty scratching up with my rocks. Why don't we take my Beetle?"

Heather led me to her brand-new green-sherbet Volks-wagen Beetle. I felt silly carrying Millie's sandwich with me, but I'd save it for the next day. They were certainly too good to just abandon.

I said, "I've never ridden in one of the new Bugs. How is it?"

She lifted the plastic red rose out of the built-in bud vase and pretended to smell it. "It's wonderful, absolutely perfect for what I need."

As she drove toward the pizzeria, I said, "Do you mind me asking how well your store does? I'm new to all this, and I've got nothing to go by."

Heather scolded me. "Harrison, there are three things you must never ask a woman: her age, her weight, and her income."

"Sorry, I was just curious."

Heather grinned. "Okay, I'll share it with you, but you can't tell a soul. Do you promise?"

"You have my word," I said.

"Last year I cleared seven figures," she said solemnly.

From selling rocks? I was in the wrong business. Heather waited a beat or two, then added with a smile, "If you don't count the decimal point, and put two of the zeros after it."

"That's cute," I said. "Mind if I steal it?"

"It's yours for the taking," she said.

I said, "Remember, dinner's on me," as we pulled into the crowded parking lot.

"Hey, I asked you. I should get to pay," Heather said.

"You bought lunch yesterday, I'll buy tonight. It's not like this is a date or anything."

Heather's face tightened for a split second, and I knew I'd stepped into it again.

"Not that I wouldn't enjoy dating you sometime," I added lamely.

It took me a second to see the smile on Heather's face. "Of course this isn't a date." She added mischievously, "I'm sure you'll take me somewhere much nicer when we start officially going out."

I started to backpedal again when she slapped my shoulder. "Harrison, you are just too easy. I've got to stop teasing you."

"I wouldn't know how to act," I said.

It looked like Belle had given me a great deal more than a business and a building full of tenants. She'd given me something much more important; a group of people who could easily become new friends.

Eight

A Slice of Heaven was hopping with customers. Since it was Saturday night, I expected the place to be swamped by teenagers, but I was surprised by the range of folks there enjoying a night out. The booths were all black vinyl, the carpeting an industrial gray, and the walls painted an audacious red. Vintage music from the jukebox barely made a dent in the clatter of conversations. Bill Haley and the Comets were rocking around the clock one minute, then Patsy Cline was belting out "Crazy" the next. The smells coming from the kitchen were no doubt part of the reason for the place's popularity. It was worth the trip even if you didn't eat anything, just to catch a whiff of that aroma.

Heather guided me to one of the only open booths, a spot far away from the jukebox, and said, "Wait right here. I'll be back in a second." She took three steps, paused, then yelled back, "What do you like on your pizza?"

"You decide. I'll eat just about anything."

Heather nodded, then came back a few minutes later after fighting through the crowd to place our order.

"So what are we having?" I asked.

"I ordered us a garbage pizza."

I smiled gently. "This place might be doing great, but they should probably work on the names of their specials."

Heather laughed, showing dimples I hadn't seen before. "Okay, they call it the Heaven Scent, but it's got everything on it they don't throw away, so I call it a garbage pizza. It doesn't sound very appetizing, does it?"

"Are you kidding me? I can't wait." The music in the background shifted to an old Frank Sinatra tune, and I said, "The musical tastes around here are eclectic, aren't they?"

Heather said, "You can request a new record for the juke-box with every tenth pizza you buy. There are only a couple of conditions, but they're written in stone. Your pick has to be from the '50s or '60s, that's the only music the owner, April May, really likes, and if you don't renew it every two months, the song gets pulled if it hasn't fallen out of the rotation by then."

"Please tell me you're kidding."

Heather said, "It's the truth. I had The Purple People Eaters on last month."

"I'm not talking about the music. Are you telling me the woman who owns this place is really named April May?"

Heather grinned and waved to an older woman standing behind the counter with an easy smile and flaming red hair. She had on an apron that said, "Kiss your Momma" and was sporting a pair of green bibbed overalls underneath it.

"What can I get you, love?" she said to Heather as the crowd parted for her when she walked toward us.

"April, I'd like you to meet Harrison Black. He was Belle's great-nephew."

April patted my shoulder. "She was a good woman, Harrison. You have my deepest sympathy."

"Thank you, ma'am."

Heather grinned, then said, "Harrison doesn't believe your name is real."

April laughed. "Oh, it's real enough. Mother wanted to name me March and make April my middle name, but Dad put his foot down. Can you imagine? I would have been March April May. That's more of a burden than any kid should have."

"So what is your middle name?" I asked.

"It's Garnet, after my grandmother. And Dad thought he was doing me a favor. There was no way I was going to go by that, so I went through school as the Calendar Girl. Now I kind of like it. It sets me apart from the rest of the herd."

There was a call for April from the counter, and she said, "Gotta go. Nice meeting you, Harrison. Come back when we have more time to chat."

As she left us, I asked, "Did Belle come here a lot?" There was so much I didn't know about my great-aunt, and talking to her friends was the only way I had left to get to know the woman she had been, not just my great-aunt.

"Oh, Belle was a huge fan of pizza. We used to eat here together just about every Saturday night." Heather paused, then added, "I wasn't going to say anything, but this is kind of in her honor. I needed something, some way to mourn, you know? Don't get me wrong, I knew Belle's wishes as well as anyone else did. The woman absolutely detested funerals. But still, I never got to say good-bye."

"I know just what you mean. I've got a candle she made. From what Eve said it was the last one she ever poured, and I've been burning it an hour a night in her memory."

Heather touched my hand. "That's the sweetest thing I've ever heard."

April joined us again at the booth, carrying a monstrous pizza in one hand and a tray holding three beers.

Heather protested, "Hey, I ordered a small pizza."

April nodded and said with a grin, "I need to take a break and get off my feet for a while, so I thought I'd join you." The pizzeria owner looked uncertain for a moment, then added, "Unless this is a date. My goodness, I've put my foot in it again, haven't I?"

Heather and I spoke simultaneously. "This isn't a date."

We stared at each other, then laughed at the same time.

April said, "Okay, I get it, no need to shout. So would you two like some company?"

I scooted over to make room for her. "That would be great."

AFTER WE ATE, I offered to pay. April looked at my money as if it were tainted with sludge. "Save it, Harrison. I just hope I get the chance to earn that and more."

"I'll definitely be back," I said, patting my stomach. I'd eaten entirely too much pizza, but the combination of good beer, better pizza and excellent conversation made me as hungry as a wolf in winter.

"That's all I need to hear," she said as she gathered up what was left of our meal. "See you all later," April said as she whisked the empty platter and mugs away.

Heather asked me if I was ready to go, and I agreed. It had been a big day, even without the robbery. As we walked out of the restaurant, Elvis was having a "Blue Christmas."

Back at River's Edge, Heather stopped the car and said, "Thanks Harrison. That was great fun."

"I should be the one thanking you," I said. "I really needed this tonight."

As she started to get out too, I said, "Hey, you don't have to walk me to my door."

Heather said with a smile, "Don't you wish. I want to go by my storage locker and get my gym bag. I'm going for a run in the morning and I usually leave my stuff here, but it's in desperate need of washing. I've been absolutely glowing lately."

"Glowing?" I asked, not sure exactly what she meant.

Heather said, "Harrison, surely you know that Southern women don't sweat. But boy, do we ever glow."

Instead of veering off to The New Age, she followed me up the steps.

"Okay, now you can't deny it. You're stalking me," I said.

"Easy, big guy, the lockers are upstairs. Didn't anybody tell you about them?"

I shook my head. "If they did, I forgot all about it. Why do you need a storage locker away from your store?"

"It was Belle's idea. There's a shower that locks and a changing area too. This way we all have a reason to say 'hi' in the mornings if we have one central place to congregate. Just about everyone here uses a locker. You need one of these to get in," she said as she held a key up.

"I'll have to get one from Pearly," I said.

"Belle had spares in her apartment. I lost mine three weeks ago and she replaced it with this new one."

Heather unlocked a door I'd ignored earlier and said, "Come on, the lockers are all in here."

She reached inside and flipped on the light switch.

Someone had gotten there before us. Every last locker had been broken into, the cleanly cut locks lying on the floor amid all the personal items that had been stored in them. The perpetrator had vandalized the contents of the lockers, smashing perfume bottles, aftershave lotion and deodorant containers among the clothes, leaving everything with a wretched smell that would take dynamite to remove.

I wanted to call Sheriff Coburn before Heather touched anything. "He may need to look for fingerprints," I said. "Don't let anyone mess with this."

I raced to Belle's apartment, dialed the sheriff's number and got him on the fifth ring.

"Coburn here," he said.

"Sheriff, there's been another break-in at River's Edge. We need you down here."

Morgan said, "Was a store hit this time?"

"It's not a shop, it's the employee locker room. The locks have all been cut and the contents thrown on the floor."

"Sounds like simple vandalism to me," the sheriff said calmly.

I said angrily, "You need a key to get in. Doesn't that tell you something?"

"Harrison, Belle herself complained to me that folks were losing their keys all the time. Most likely some kid found one and thought he'd make a quick score."

"Did this 'kid' also just happen to have a set of bolt cutters on him? Those locks were cleanly sheered off."

"You'd be surprised by the kind of junk we pull off them. It's likely a harmless stunt. I can't imagine anyone crazy enough to store valuables up there."

"Does that mean you're not coming?" I couldn't believe his unwillingness to investigate.

"Gee, Harrison, I'd love to drop everything to come over there and pat your hand, but I just had a hit-and-run on Elm, and I was kind of on my way over to that."

"At least stop by on your way back to the station," I said, understanding his position a little better.

"Clean up the mess, post a note about the keys and forget it, Harrison."

When I walked back to the locker room, Heather asked, "Is he coming?"

I shook my head. "No, he claims he's too busy."

"Typical," Heather snorted. "We're not all that high a priority for him, especially now that Belle's gone. They were friends, but since she died, I haven't seen him around River's Edge."

I admitted, "He came by to offer his condolences, but everyone else was gone."

"Well, he gets a point for that, I guess." She scanned the mess and asked, "So what do we do now?"

"I guess I'll clean it up," I said as I started shaking broken glass out of a shirt on the floor.

As we worked side by side, Heather said with disgust, "I just can't imagine someone doing this. What were they looking for?"

"The same thing they were hunting for in Belle's apartment," I said, forgetting for a moment that Heather was still one of my suspects.

"Harrison, I loved Belle dearly, but I can't imagine that she owned anything worth stealing, can you?"

"Something's going on around here," I said, "and if the police aren't going to do anything about it, I'm going to have to find out myself."

Heather swept up the last of the glass, and I finished putting the clothing in an empty box I'd found on top of one of the lockers.

I said, "I'll wash this mess and bring it back tomorrow."

She took the box from me and said, "You're not going to ruin your washer. I'll stop off at the Laundromat on the way home. I've got a load of my own to do, so it's no problem."

"Are you sure?" I said. "I hate to ask you to do it."

"You didn't ask. I volunteered. Good night, Harrison. What can I say? It's been interesting."

"I can't argue with that. Thanks again. For everything."

After Heather was gone, I wrote a note explaining what had happened and taped it to the front door of the locker room. At least that way no one would get a shock going in unprepared.

Back in Belle's apartment, finally settling in for the night, I double-bolted the new locks on the door. The place still didn't feel all that safe to me until I lit Belle's candle. There was something about watching that flickering flame that soothed my nerves and eased my spirit. It was almost as if I could feel Belle's very real presence there with me. The cinnamon in the air made me long for one more batch of Snickerdoodles and a quiet afternoon with my great-aunt. By the time the candle had burned its allotted hour, I was no closer to solving the mystery of the most recent break-in than I had been when I started.

But I did feel more at peace than I had in a very long time. After I snuffed out the wick, I couldn't keep myself from wondering why someone had so methodically sheared the locks off every locker, and then make such a horrible mess of the contents. Was it out of frustration, much as Belle's break-in had been? The two incidents certainly looked like they were committed by the same vandal. But was the carnage a true reaction from the perpetrator, or was it just a clever cover-up to hide a more calculated search? Either way, I couldn't help wondering if the thief had found what was being so diligently sought, or if we were going to have more robberies at River's Edge.

AS A GENERAL rule, I always slept in on Sundays; it was a bit of a ritual for me. So I was stunned to find that it was barely past seven the next morning when I rolled out of bed, fully and completely awake. I knew myself well enough to realize that it wouldn't do me a bit of good to try to go back to sleep. We didn't open At Wick's End until two on Sunday afternoons, so that gave me a lot of time on my hands. I thought about all the things I might do, from renting a movie, playing tennis with my friend Wayne, or curling up on the couch leisurely going through the Sunday paper.

What I did was get dressed, grab a quick bowl of cereal, and head down to the shop so I could get an early jump on things at the candle shop. Running a business was quite a bit different from working for one. Sure, it was great being my own boss, but in many ways, I was turning out to be harder on myself than any of my previous employers ever had been.

And I was determined to make up for my mistake yesterday, even if it meant working every minute I was awake until I found a way to repay the store the cost of my carelessness.

"DON'T YOU EVER take any time off," Eve asked when she walked in later that day. I held up one of the books I'd been studying most of the morning and into the afternoon. "It's the only way I'm going to be able to pitch in and do my share of the work around here. There's a lot to learn, but I can't keep running the cash register forever."

Eve nodded. "I must say, I'm impressed with your diligence in learning about candles."

I swallowed, then said, "Don't be too impressed yet. There's something I have to confess to you. I did something really stupid yesterday, Eve." I proceeded to tell her what had happened with the deposits, and her lips pursed into a pair of grim lines.

"The checks were lost as well," she asked.

"No, they were still in the truck, scattered all over the floor, but they were fine. I made out a new deposit slip and dropped off what was left at the bank. Eve, it was a mistake that won't happen again."

She nodded. "Sometimes the only way we learn is the hard way." If there was any scolding in her voice, she did her best to hide it.

I felt a burden lift as we moved on to a discussion about the best way to pour candles, a technique I was very eager to learn. If I was being honest with myself, I was more concerned about telling Eve what I'd done than losing all that cash.

Eve said, "Well, why don't we straighten up the store and get ready for our customers?"

"I'm all for that," I said.

As we put away the books and supplies that I'd pulled out from our inventory to study, I said in passing, "By the way, somebody broke into the lockers upstairs last night and wrecked the whole communal room."

Eve dropped the tin candle mold she was holding, and it clattered to the floor. "Oh, no," she said, looking paler than I'd ever seen her.

"There's nothing that you can do now," I said. "Heather and I cleaned everything up after we discovered what had happened. She even washed the soiled clothes. I'm afraid some of the spilled perfume and aftershave got on them during the break-in. They're all sitting on the table, neat and pressed and ready to claim, if you had any clothes in your locker." We had placed the other miscellaneous items we'd been able to salvage on the table as well. A couple of things had to be thrown away, but there were surprisingly few items that were totally lost.

Eve nearly knocked me into a shelf as she brushed past me heading for the front door. I understood why she was so upset. It's a violation when someone paws through your things, an offense much more serious than a few broken bottles and a pile of soiled clothes. The thief takes your sense of security from you, and that's a much more terrible crime than mere property loss.

When she returned ten minutes later, Eve had a frightened look about her.

"What is it," I asked, concerned that something else may have happened to her.

"Harrison, this used to be such a safe place," she said.

"And it will be again," I said, trying to soothe her. "The sheriff believes that what happened upstairs was just a random act of violence." I didn't add that I was of a different opinion entirely, since I was trying to ease her mind, not add to her worries.

Eve said, "Harrison, I'm sorry, but I don't think I'll be able to work today," as she grabbed her coat.

"I can't do this without you," I said. Surely she was over-reacting, but what could I do? I couldn't very well chain her to the cash register to make her stay.

"Close up then. I can't stay here, not today."

As she reached for the door, I said, "You're coming back tomorrow, aren't you?"

She didn't answer as she bolted out, slamming the door behind her.

I couldn't help wondering if the break-in had truly thrown her into such a panic, or if someone might have found something in her particular locker that she hadn't wanted discovered.

I WENT SO far as to make up a CLOSED sign for the front door when I decided to try running At Wick's End by myself. What was the worst thing that could happen; I wouldn't be able to help a customer? So, they could come back another day and Eve could help them, if she showed up. It was my store, blast it all, and I wasn't about to let anything stand between me and my customers. If they went to all the trouble of coming down to River's Edge, then the least I could do was keep my store open for them. I knew how complicated candlemaking could be, I'd read just enough to realize how much I didn't know about the operation, but I'd do my best and above all, I'd be honest with whoever walked through my door. I hadn't overtly lied to Mrs. Jorgenson, but I hadn't done anything to correct her mistaken belief that I was some kind of candlemaking wizard, either. I wish I could have believed somewhere in my heart that the threat to the candle shop's bottom line had nothing to do with the decision to keep my novice status to myself, but I couldn't begin to justify that stand.

I tore the homemade sign up, threw the pieces into the trash can, and turned on all the lights. At Wick's End was open for business. Whether I was ready for my customers or not.

MY AFTERNOON WENT better than I had any right to expect. I couldn't have done a full shift alone, but in the six hours I stayed open I managed to make quite a dent in the cash I'd lost the day before.

Besides, keeping the shop open had given me a sense of control over my life that I'd been sorely missing since Belle had dropped the entire complex into my lap.

Still, I hated the prospect of facing a full day without Eve there to bail me out if I needed it. I managed to buy some time with a few customers until Eve's return, if she came back at all, but I handled more problems than I had any reason to expect during the course of the day.

Drifting off to sleep that night with a candlemaking book tented across my chest, I couldn't help wondering if what had happened to Belle was related to Eve's reaction to the locker room break-in upstairs.

If she came in to work tomorrow, I promised myself, I'd ask her about it.

Nine

EVE didn't say a word the next morning until she opened the cash register and looked at the tape from the previous day's report. I'd been tiptoeing around her from the moment she'd walked in, dying to ask what had set her off the day before but afraid to lose her for another day, or worse yet, for good.

She studied the register tape for a minute, then finally said, "You opened yesterday after all?"

I said, "I was here anyway, and besides, I figured if I got too far in over my head, you could bail me out today. I did okay."

She took that in, studied the tape again, then said grudgingly, "You did better than okay. From these figures, I'd say you managed pretty well on your own, Harrison."

"I didn't answer everybody's questions, but a couple of folks promised to come back today to talk to you."

She looked as if she was going to cry, then mumbled something I couldn't hear.

"Pardon," I said gently, "I missed that."

"I said I'm sorry I let you down," Eve said forcibly. "I should have been here."

"Hey, you needed some time to yourself," I said. "I could tell the break-in upset you."

"Harrison, I never would have done that to Belle, just abandoned her like that."

"It's okay, believe me." I glanced at the clock. "But I've got to tell you, I'm really glad you're here today. I've got a ton of things going on, and I couldn't manage without you."

Eve said, "That's right, Mrs. Jorgenson is coming in for her first lesson today, isn't she?"

"Don't forget, I'm meeting with our bookkeeper before that. I hate to walk out on you just before we open, but I've got to have this meeting with Ann Marie Hart if I'm ever going to figure out our accounting system."

Eve said, "You won't be bailing out on me, that's a part of store business." She added with a grin, "Even if you were, that would make us even."

Two minutes after nine, a rail-thin blonde with a dizzying smile walked in, a stack of books and journals balanced under one arm and a thick briefcase dangling from the other. She needed a shopping cart for all the things she was carrying.

"Hey Eve," she said with a thick Tennessee accent that was uniquely its own. She plopped the books down on the counter and extended her hand to me. "You must be Harrison. Or would you prefer Mr. Black?"

"Harrison's fine."

She nodded. "Then I'm Ann Marie. Shall we get down to business?"

"I'm ready if you are."

We walked back to the office, and Ann Marie said, "Harrison, I've been up since 4 AM going over everything just to make sure I had my ducks all in a row. Let's teach you about business for At Wick's End."

As she spread her books across the desk Eve and I

shared in the office, I said, "There's something you should know right up front. All the cash is gone from Saturday's deposit."

The air went out of Ann Marie as she slumped against the desk. "Which is it, gambling, booze, drugs or fast women, Harrison?" she asked in a dogged voice.

"Pardon me?"

Ann Marie said with a sigh, "It will help me if I know exactly what problem we're dealing with here. Now I can put you on an allowance if you're willing, and I'll make arrangements to come by and do the deposit every night myself. That is if you're interested in saving this business and not running it into the ground so you can go out and raise a little mischief."

"Hang on, Ann Marie, you've got me wrong. I don't have any bad habits, at least not any of the ones you mentioned. The worst thing I do is drink right out of the milk carton without bothering with a glass. Okay, I've been known to dog-ear the page of a book now and then, but I'm trying to break that habit, believe me."

"So what happened to the cash?"

I said, "I was boneheaded enough to leave it in my truck when I went into the library, and somebody broke the window and stole it."

Ann Marie looked thrilled by the revelation. "So you're just careless. We can work on that. I've had a bad run of luck lately with my clients, and I'm glad you're not going to be adding to the mix. I just found out one of my clients in Conover is drinking his way into an early grave and stealing from his business to cover things up with his wife. I don't even want to talk about Max Bleeker being murdered. I don't know how I'll ever get over that."

"Who's Max Bleeker?"

She said, "He ran his own jewelry store." Ann Marie sighed. "But let's stick to your problems, Harrison. We've got enough on our plate here without dragging the rest of this part of North Carolina in on things."

"Ann Marie, I've beaten myself up about what happened more than anyone else could. Mr. Young told me how thin a tightrope I'm walking here. It won't happen again."

She said, "I believe you, Harrison. It makes a difference when it's your own money, doesn't it? I don't know that things are all that dire, though; there's a real chance you'll be able to make this work. That's funny, Lucas isn't usually so cynical. Our bad streak of luck must be getting to him too." She clapped her hands together once, then said, "Now let's take a look at the books and teach you the ins and outs of this candle shop."

BY THE TIME we were finished, my head was swimming with numbers, schedules, tax payments and property valuations. I stood and stretched. "Bottom line, how are we doing?"

"Getting by, I'd say," she said after thinking about it a moment. "You're doing about as well as can be expected here, given the fact that Belle didn't believe in advertising. There's enough to pay Eve and keep your inventory going, shoot, we could probably bump you a few dollars above what Belle was pulling in, but I wouldn't be planning any trips to Europe if I were you."

"As long as we're not bankrupt, I'm happy. You should know I'm planning an ad campaign myself, and we've also got a star customer who should help the bottom line."

Ann Marie smiled and said, "Don't tell me, Mrs. Jorgenson has finally discovered At Wick's End."

"How'd you know that?"

"Oh, please, I do the books for several crafters around here. Mrs. Jorgenson is a legend in your circles. I'm glad things are going well for you."

"As well as can be expected, given the circumstances. As long as you're using black ink and not red, I'm thrilled."

Ann Marie said, "You're easy to please, aren't you?

Do you have any questions I can answer in the meantime?"

"Yes. When's payday? I've got enough to hold me for a while, but it might help to know how long my nest egg has to stretch before I draw a salary."

She reached into her purse and pulled out two yellow envelopes. "I love getting questions I can answer. I come by every other Monday with your checks. This is the good Monday." She handed me both checks, then added, "Your draw is tied into the store's profits, so it varies. Eve gets a straight salary. If that doesn't work for you, we can always change it. Now if you'll give Eve's check to her, I'll get over to The Yarn Barn. I'm meeting Lucas Young for a counseling session. We can offer a lot of advice as a package deal, and a great many folks take advantage of it."

"Thanks Ann Marie, I appreciate the lesson today."

She smiled broadly. "You're paying for it, Harrison. Call me any time. Except after 5 PM, or on weekends. I'm off on Wednesdays, so that's no good either. Sometimes I baby-sit for my sister Sarah Ann's three kids, so I'm not always home then. I never answer the phone before 8:30 AM, that's when I'm working on everyone's books. But other than that, I'm all yours."

I chuckled softly to myself as she left. Ann Marie was something entirely unto herself, and though she'd painted a dark picture of my earnings, it wasn't as bleak as Lucas Young had implied.

I peeked at my check, not sure what to expect. I was a little disappointed at first by the amount, then I realized I was my own landlord, so rent and utilities were covered from that account, a sizable expense I would be exempted from. The amount of the check certainly gave me incentive to see how I could raise profits around the candle shop, since my pay was tied directly to it. It was a fair way to do it, and I was glad Belle had chosen to set it up that way.

* * *

AS I HANDED Eve her check, I asked, "Is Mrs. Jorgenson here yet?"

"No, but I've heard she's always punctual. Are you ready for your lesson?"

I ticked the steps off in my mind, fairly confident I could follow the correct procedures in the right order. "I think so."

Eve added, "While we're waiting for her to arrive, there's something I need to discuss with you."

"What's that?" I asked as I checked over the supplies I'd laid out for the day's lesson.

"It's about yesterday," she said hesitantly.

"There's nothing to discuss," I said. "You deserve some time off now and then."

Eve snorted. "I wasn't taking a vacation day, and you know it. I came unglued when I heard about the break-in upstairs, and I left you here alone. It was unforgivable."

"It's already forgotten," I said.

Eve pushed, "It rattled me, Harrison, and there was no reason for it. Belle's death has shaken me more than I've been willing to admit." She took a deep breath, then said, "I'm dealing with it, though. Work will help."

A thought suddenly struck me. "Eve, how many hours do you work in a normal week?"

Instead of offering a direct answer to my question, she said, "I don't mind coming in, Harrison. You need help until you get your feet on the ground here."

"I need to know. What's a typical week for you?"

Eve said, "I usually work three full days a week, every afternoon, plus one or two evenings and every other weekend. But nobody expects you to take over the shop until you learn the ins and outs of the candle business, Harrison."

"I'd appreciate it if you could work with me this week, but starting next Monday we go back to your old schedule, the one you had with Belle."

"If it's the money, we can consider part of it as volunteer work," Eve said frostily.

"I'm not going to lie to you and tell you money's got

nothing to do with it, but that's just part of it. I need to learn to stand on my own two feet here. I'm going to make mistakes, I fully expect that, but the more I work the store on my own, the quicker life around here can get back to normal. I do have one favor to ask, though."

"You know I'm happy to oblige," she said.

"Keep teaching me the processes. I'm having a wonderful time learning, but I know more than anyone how weak my background is in the basics."

Eve offered one of her rare smiles. "You've got a knack for it, Harrison. I can't tell you how happy I am you enjoy it. Belle would have been so pleased."

The overhead bell chimed, and I saw Mrs. Jorgenson coming toward me, a resolute expression on her face. So much for "Feel Good" Monday.

"Good morning," I said as I led Mrs. J back to the classroom. "Are you ready to get started?"

"Absolutely. I've turned off my telephone, so we won't be disturbed this time."

I got her started with sheets of wax and wicks, and to my chagrin, she was nearly perfect from the start. I had counted on spending an hour having her roll and reroll her candles, but I had to admit, her first attempt was better formed than my last. How in the world was I going to keep her occupied now?

She studied the results, then said, "Surely there's something else we can do with these sheets."

I was suddenly very thankful I'd put so much time in preparing for this lesson. "We're just getting started," I said. I reached behind me and retrieved an array of cookie cutter molds with waxy edges. "Let's try your hand at some different shapes."

I grabbed another batch of various colored wax sheets I'd retrieved from the storeroom and ripped the packs open.

As I fanned the sheets out on the table, I said, "There are several ways you can do this. Cut-outs all from the same color look nice, but complementary colors are attractive too. Why don't you cut six pieces of the same shape and we'll make a candle with them."

Mrs. Jorgenson opted for a maple leaf cutter and quickly cut out six leafy imprints.

"Now measure out your wick, put it between two leaves, then keep sandwiching the cut-outs evenly. Your goal here is to keep the wick in the center of the candle."

She did as she was told, then delicately pressed them all together.

"That was easy," she said as the leaf-candle fell apart, the wick lying on the table like a discarded string.

"What happened?" she asked, studying the fallen sections.

Fortunately, my first cut-out candle had done the same thing, so I knew just what to do. "Put it all back together, press firmly this time, then we'll try adding a little heat."

I took a blow-dryer out of one of the cabinets and gave the leaf a good blast of heated air around the edges after she reassembled it. "Pinch the edges together like this. It gives the candle a more rounded look." It held together this time, and Mrs. Jorgenson looked pleased with the results.

"I'd like to do another one on my own now."

She chose a club shape from one of the card cutters and opted for a lavender wax. This attempt was a great improvement over the last, and by the time our session was over, she'd made nine different shapes and seven rolled candles.

I collected them for her, carefully wrapping each candle individually before placing it in her bag. I still couldn't tell from her expression or demeanor whether she had enjoyed the process or not. It was possible my star student had taken her first and last lesson all at the same time.

As we walked out to the cash register, Mrs. Jorgenson waved a hand at Eve and said, "I need a selection of colors from your stock of sheet wax. Let's say three packs of each."

"We have sixteen colors in stock," Eve said.

Mrs. Jorgenson thought about it a moment, then said, "Is that all? We'd better make it six packs of each then, I have a great deal of work ahead of me." She frowned, then added, "I just had a thought. I'll need three sets of every cutter you have in stock."

I was standing just behind her. "You only need one set of cutters."

Eve shot me a dirty look as Mrs. Jorgenson turned to me and said, "I've decided to give two sets to my nieces as presents." While Eve disappeared into the storeroom to put the order together, Mrs. Jorgenson handed me her credit card. "Why don't you handle the billing while we wait?"

I totaled up her bill including the merchandise Eve was collecting and the supplies we'd used in our lesson today. Before I ran it through our system, I said, "Excuse me a moment, would you?"

"Certainly," she said. "That will give me the opportunity to browse a little."

I found Eve quickly going through the boxes in the storeroom, making up Mrs. Jorgenson's order.

She brushed a wisp of hair out of her face. "Is something wrong? Did she change her mind?"

"Keep pulling stock," I said as I helped her with a heavier box off the top shelf. A wave of anxiety ran through me when I realized I was standing on the exact spot where Belle's body had been discovered, but I fought it back.

"Why are you here, then? I can handle this, Harrison. Honestly, you shouldn't leave her out there alone. She might leave."

"Right now I doubt I could get her out of the store with a crowbar; that woman's got the candlemaking fever worse than I do. I need to know what we charge for private lessons," I said.

Eve said, "I haven't a clue. I know what the group lessons run, but we've never had an individual demand personal instruction before."

"Let's double the regular fee then. What do you say?"

Eve frowned and bit her lower lip. "I honestly don't know. We don't want to alienate her."

I laughed. "The lady is determined to learn. Why not charge her for the privilege?"

"It's your shop, Harrison."

"Double it is, then."

When I got back from the storeroom, I couldn't find Mrs. Jorgenson anywhere. Oh, no. I shouldn't have left her alone after all. Then I saw her head appear above a shelf full of copper cookie cutters, a dozen or so in her hands. "I'll take these as well."

I added them to her total, along with the amount, astronomical in hindsight, I was charging her for lessons. Seeing it on paper gave me a bout of cold feet. Would she balk at the fee and walk out? I mentioned the total to her casually, fighting to keep the jitters out of my voice.

Her only comment was, "That sounds quite reasonable," and I suddenly wondered if I'd charged her enough. Oh, well, it was too late now.

Eve began carrying boxes out of the storeroom, and Mrs. Jorgenson gave her the remote control to her trunk. I said, "Hang on a second, I can take care of that."

"I don't mind," Eve said as she disappeared outside.

I handed Mrs. Jorgenson her credit card as well as the receipt for her to sign, then gave her the other copy. "Would you like to set up your next lesson now?"

She nodded. "Let's say the same time next week, shall we? I plan on devoting this week to rolling."

She started for the door, then said, "You know, I'm quite impressed with your ability to teach candlemaking. It's as if you still remember what it was like to learn it for the first time."

"Thanks," I said.

"You have a feel for the wax, don't you?"

"I'd like to think so," I admitted. "You've got a real knack yourself."

When Eve came back inside a minute later, there was a bemused smile on her face. "What's so funny?" I asked.

"She actually tipped me," Eve said, holding a ten up in the air. "Did she give you one too?"

"Not a chance. It looks like you're buying lunch," I said.

Eve tucked the money in her blouse pocket, then studied

the bill I'd made out. She gasped when she saw the amount. I said, "I didn't charge enough, did I?"

"Enough? Harrison, that total I gave you was for an entire class of five. You charged her much too much."

I grinned. "Funny, she thought it was quite reasonable."

Eve still looked troubled. "I still think it's too much."

I said, "Then I'll give her a break on her supplies the next time she comes in, but I don't think it was a mistake. I'm telling you, she didn't bat an eye."

"Let's not try to make up all of our losses on her," Eve said softly. "No matter how tempting it might be."

I was about to respond when Pearly came in, a scowl on his face.

"What's wrong," I asked him, not sure I wanted to know the answer.

Ten

PEARLY said, "I was just upstairs at my locker. Do you mind telling me what happened? It smells like a perfume factory blew up in there, and all my possessions are scattered about on a table. Are we having an unscheduled yard sale no one mentioned to me, Harrison?"

Eve looked flustered by the comment and said curtly, "I need to tidy up the back room, if you'll excuse me."

After she was gone, Pearly asked, "Was it something I said?"

"No, she's been like that since yesterday." I took a deep breath, then said, "We had another break-in the night before last. Somebody went through the locks with a bolt cutter and dumped everything out onto the floor."

Pearly frowned. "There was a bottle of aftershave my granddaughter bought me for Christmas. I suppose it's all gone as well, isn't it?"

I nodded sadly. "I'm sorry, there were several broken bottles in the mess."

He brightened for a moment, then said, "I suppose that's the silver lining in all this then. I detested the concoction, and now I can honestly say that it was destroyed by vandals. That should save me until next Christmas, though I can't imagine what that will bring; my granddaughter has a rather eccentric taste in scents. Do the police have any idea who could have done it?"

"Sheriff Coburn's too busy to deal with it," I said, trying to hide the ire in my voice.

Pearly nodded. "I don't doubt that. Rumor has it that he's under a great deal of pressure from the mayor and town council about the murder in the jewelry store, Harrison. It most likely makes this appear to be nothing more than the act of a juvenile delinquent."

"You don't believe that any more than I do," I said. "There's no way this could be random, not with what happened in Belle's apartment. Besides, who carries bolt cutters around with them on the off chance they'll be able to use them?"

"There are odd powers at work here, Harrison. It would be in your best interest to keep your eyes open and your back protected."

I asked softly, "Pearly, is there something you know that you're not telling me?"

"Nothing concrete, Harrison, but I suspect we're not done with this, and I've learned to trust my instincts over the years."

After the handyman was gone, I decided to see what was keeping Eve so enthralled back in the storeroom. "Everything under control back here?" I asked.

"We'll need to reorder our sheet wax kits, Mrs. Jorgenson nearly wiped us out. Is Pearly gone?"

I nodded. "Listen, I've been thinking about it. If you honestly think I cheated Mrs. Jorgenson on her lessons, I'd be happy to give her a rebate the next time she comes in."

She shook her head. "No, I overreacted. Belle was always chastising me for looking out for the customer more than I did the shop. It is a business, after all, and we must run at a profit if we want to continue. I believe you charged just the right amount, Harrison. I'm certain Belle would have approved."

"Okay, we're set then. And now we have a fee schedule for private lessons, if it should ever come up again."

Eve laughed. "Oh, I doubt we'll get many Mrs. Jorgensons. They are a rarity in our circles."

"Hey, we never thought we'd get one, remember?" My stomach rumbled, and I said, "Do you want to go to lunch first, or should I?"

She glanced at her watch. "You go. I like eating later, if it's all the same to you."

"Good enough. I'll see you in a little bit."

I headed over to Millie's and picked up a sandwich and a Coke to go. I wasn't in the mood for company after the morning I'd had. The lesson had gone well with Mrs. Jorgenson, and my meeting with Ann Marie had been quite illuminating, but I just wanted to be by myself, if only for a half an hour or so. I was discovering that part of owning a store was the fact that the store owned part of me. As soon as Eve went back to her regular hours, I'd be tied to it as if I had a toddler of my own, and I wasn't sure I liked that feeling.

Pearly was in Millie's standing near the counter, and I nodded to him as I placed my order. I half expected him to say something else about the trouble at River's Edge, but one look into his eyes told me that he was in no more of a mood to discuss it than I was. As Millie started making my sandwich, Pearly said, "I was just sharing with Millie news of my recent day trip to the dog park to wager on a few of the tail-waggers with a lady friend from Charlotte. On the tour bus, I spent most of the ride enjoying myself analyzing the folks there from Micah's Ridge. You wouldn't believe it, it was like a roster of Who's Who in local society. The mayor was there, Lucas Young sitting right beside him, why, I even saw Clara Ridgway from the Junior League pretending she was going to visit a cousin I know for a fact she doesn't have. Watching them squirm was more fun than the gambling." It was obvious he was trying to lighten the mood, but I wasn't interested. I had too much on my mind.

Millie returned with my sandwich, and Pearly said, "Care to join me, Harrison? I'm getting ready to order myself."

"Thanks, but I'm going to take advantage of this day while I can."

I took the sandwich and started for the steps that led to the water, but it was too close to River's Edge, and for once I just wanted to get away from the complex. I walked along the riverbank for ten minutes until I got to a spot that offered an uninterrupted view of the water and was away from the highway as well. A torn section of newspaper skittered in the wind close enough for me to grab it as I sat, and as I ate, I perused the old headlines, reading the story of the robbery/murder that had Micah's Ridge in such an uproar.

It seemed a thief had entered Bleeker Jewelers just after they opened for business that morning. The thief must have known enough to steal the videotape from the security camera along with a great many diamonds, so the police initially thought it might be a disgruntled former employee who knew about the security system. Bleeker's was a family operation, though, and the few employees outside the family had solid alibis. No one knew why the thief had turned murderer. Bleeker had gone against his own policy and had opened the store that day by himself. He'd always told his employees that if a robber came in not to be a hero; jewels could be replaced, lives could not. It was a pity the man had ignored his own advice.

I crumpled the paper up and tossed it into my now empty lunch bag, wondering what could drive someone to commit murder.

Then I started thinking about Belle, and I was more confused than ever. Certainly she wasn't the easiest woman in the world to get along with at times, there was too much salt and vinegar in her, but could someone have possibly been driven to murder her? Could it have been another theft gone bad, like the jewelry store? One look at the meager till of At Wick's End would cancel that notion, unless someone thought a candlemaking shop took in a great deal more than it did. That started me thinking about the break-in of the truck. Was there any way the theft of the cash from my Saturday deposit was tied into Belle's death? No, it was probably just my boneheadedness that had led to that particular crime. So if Belle hadn't been killed for money or passion, why had she been murdered? Did she know something she shouldn't have? What in the world could that crusty old lady know that might get her killed?

I was no closer to an answer when I finished my meal than I had been from the start. A quick glance at my watch showed that I'd overstayed my lunch hour by ten minutes. As I gathered up my trash and headed back, I smiled when I realized no one would be able to dock my wages but me.

Lucas Young was there waiting for me at the candle shop when I got back.

"What brings you to At Wick's End?" I asked.

"This isn't a business call. I just wanted to see how you were settling in. Are there any problems with the store, or the building itself, for that matter?"

I wasn't about to admit the cash theft, not directly, at any rate. There was no need to mention the additional break-ins, either. Frankly, I didn't want the word getting around Micah's Ridge that bad things were happening at River's Edge. "We've had a few bumps in the road, but things are settling down now."

"Good to know. Well, if you need an ear to bend, I'm available."

I shook his hand. "Thanks, I appreciate that."

Belle certainly did have a way with people. I didn't know many lawyers willing to make house calls just to check in like that. It was more a testament to her life than any eulogy could have been.

The rest of the day was fairly quiet, with a steady stream of customers interspersed with lulls that allowed me to clean up the classroom. Mrs. Jorgenson had left quite a wake of discarded wax from her lesson. Worse yet, some of it had hit the floor and had been stepped on, making it a pain to remove. I was suddenly happy with the high rates I'd charged her as I scraped fragments off the floor with a putty knife.

Eve left a few minutes early to go by the bank in order to cash her paycheck, and I decided to close the store myself and join her.

"Where are you going?" she asked me as I followed her to the door.

"I thought I'd go by the bank too."

Eve said, "Harrison, we are open till six. Our customers rely on that."

"Come on, nobody's going to have a candlemaking emergency," I said. "What chance is there that a few minutes is really going to matter?"

"If you insist, I'll stay and you can go."

She was worse than my mother when it came to guilt. "No, I had plenty of time to go at lunch. I'll go tomorrow. I still think we'd be safe shutting down early."

Before the last word was out of my mouth, the door chimed and an older woman with the most marvelous silver hair hurried in. "I'm making a centerpiece for my party and I ran out of wax," she said, nearly out of breath. "Thank goodness you're still here."

Eve buried her gloating enough to wave good-bye as I waited on our last customer of the day. I should have gone to the bank earlier, but I'd forgotten all about it. That meant canned soup and another sandwich for dinner.

Tomorrow, I promised myself, I'd make it a point to cash my check so I could stock my larder upstairs. As much as I enjoyed Millie's food, eating at The Crocked Pot would bankrupt me before long.

I finished the deposit slip after ringing up the centerpiece emergency and did a quick check of the inventory levels. We were going to have to order soon, and I didn't have a clue how to go about it. I made a note to ask Eve about the process in the morning, my list of questions for her growing instead of shrinking. I didn't have the slightest idea how I'd manage without her once she went back to her regular hours.

THAT EVENING, I had just finished eating my soup and sandwich in my apartment when there was a knock at my door. I peered through the peephole and found Heather on the other side.

"It's too late to invite me out," I said with a grin as I opened the door, "I just finished eating."

The levity left me the second I saw the expression on her face. "What's wrong, Heather?"

She held fiercely to a tabby cat as she said, "My mom's in the hospital, and I've got to go be with her. Harrison, I need a huge favor."

"Anything," I said before I noticed the litter box and carrier off to one side.

"Can you watch Esmeralda for me while I'm gone? My dad can't tolerate cats. I don't know what I'm going to do. Mrs. Quimby can't take her, her husband's deathly allergic. You aren't, are you? My friend Sally was going to watch her for me, but she's out of town on a photo shoot."

"Is she a model," I asked, trying to buy some time to deal with Heather's request.

"No, she's a photographer, one of the best around here. I know I'm babbling, but I'm worried about my mother. So could you? Please?" Heather looked as if she was on the brink of breaking into tears.

What was one night? "Okay, I'll do it."

The relief on her face was instantaneous. "What a relief. Thank you, Harrison, I don't know what I would have done if you hadn't said yes. I don't know when I'll be back," she added as she thrust Esmeralda into my arms. The cat had other ideas, executing a remarkable spin that would have done an Olympic diver proud, then scampered into my apartment.

"She feels at home here. Belle used to keep her for me now and then." Heather added, "She won't be any trouble at all, I promise. I fed her a few minutes ago. Oh, dear, do you know about litter boxes?"

"Don't worry about Esmeralda, my girlfriend in college had a cat, so I know what to do." I didn't add the fact that Janie's cat Mr. Fluffy had hated me from the beginning, jealous of my presence and the attention I diverted from him. I had known better than to give her an ultimatum. We were clearly through, but before I could break it off, she dumped me. It appeared that Mr. Fluffy was the only male in her life, and I wasn't even in the running for second place.

"This is so wonderful of you," Heather said.

A thought suddenly occurred to me. "Who's going to run your store while you're gone?"

"Mrs. Quimby's going to do it. Don't worry, she's got all of that covered. I'll be back as soon as I can." Heather reached up and kissed me on the cheek, then hurried away before I had a chance to change my mind.

IT TOOK ME ten minutes to find Esmeralda once Heather was gone. I finally found her on the bookshelf, curled up in front of Belle's Agatha Christie collection. I spoke with her a few minutes, offered my hand, then tried to stroke her, but she was in no mood to be social. That suited me fine. I'd feed her, even change her litter box, but that was going to be the extent of it.

After rinsing my bowl, I picked my book up and started back in on it. Dame Agatha was as mesmerizing as ever, and I wanted to get back to her tale.

Fifteen minutes later I heard a soft thump on the hardwood floor. I pretended to ignore the sound, watching Esmeralda out of the corner of my eye as she slowly stalked toward me. After sniffing the air, she pounced on the couch beside me, then somehow managed to slide up under my book without the slightest bit of noticeable effort. It was almost as if my temporary roommate had been born without bones.

I started to stroke her fur, but she moved away before I could manage it. This relationship wasn't going to be any easier than the one I'd had with Mr. Fluffy.

Reading wasn't possible with the cat on my chest, and Esmeralda was in no mood to just hang out with me. I was tired anyway. It had been a big day. Heather had supplied a cat bed, so I laid it out in the living room, then went into the bedroom and closed the door. Two minutes after I shut the door, there was the most pitiful mewling outside.

"Go to sleep," I said through the wood, but the noise just grew louder.

"All right, you win. You can have your bed in here." It appeared that it was the only way I was going to get any sleep. Esmeralda seemed pitifully grateful when I opened the door. She circled the room while I brought her bed in and put it at the foot of mine. As she settled in for the night, I turned off the light and tried to put aside the thoughts scrambling through my mind. The same time last week I'd been in an entirely different job and apartment, my great-aunt Belle was still alive, and I hadn't been around a cat for a dozen years. It was ironic that I'd been looking for a change in my life not all that long ago.

It was a perfect example of being careful what you wished for; it just might come true.

Eleven

I woke up the next morning with an anvil on my chest. At least that's what it felt like to me. It took me a few seconds to realize that sometime during the night Esmeralda had moved from her bed to mine. Evidently the mattress had been too soft for her.

"Okay, rise and shine," I said as I gently lifted her off me. There are ways to hold a cat, and then there are ways to lose a hand. Janie had taught me how to hold Mr. Fluffy, though he'd been indignant about the whole procedure. Sometime during the night Esmeralda had accepted me as a surrogate, so she appeared to put up with my clumsy movements. Any port in the storm, I guessed, even for a cat.

Esmeralda studied me as I got dressed and ate breakfast. I tried to offer her food, but she insisted on observing me instead of eating. I couldn't imagine what she found all that fascinating.

I was still wondering what to do with her, whether to banish her to the bathroom or try to take her to the candle shop with me when there was a knock at my door. I opened it to find a sprightly little woman who immediately identified herself as Mrs. Quimby. She scooped Esmeralda up as the cat trotted over to her.

"Hello, princess," she said to the cat before she had another word for me. "Heather asked me to collect her majesty, I hope you don't mind. Esmeralda here is a fierce watch-cat for The New Age." She made eye contact with me as she added, "My Herbert is deathly allergic, else the princess would have spent the night with me. Did you two get along all right?"

"We did fine," I said. "Have you spoken to Heather this morning?"

"Oh my, yes. She knows I keep an insomniac's hours, late to bed and early to rise. Honestly, I just don't seem to sleep much anymore. Be happy for the hours of peaceful slumber you get, young man, they are a true gift from above."

"How is her mother doing," I asked.

"Much better. Heather's hoping to be back here by tomorrow night."

It appeared Esmeralda and I would be roomies for at least one more night then. "Good enough. Do you want to drop her off here after you close the shop? I've got some errands to run, but I should be back by seven." The New Age ran odder hours than At Wick's End, open on a schedule I couldn't figure out even after studying the posted times on the door.

"That would be lovely," Mrs. Quimby said. "It will give the princess and me time to commune."

"Don't let me keep you," I said as I led them out the door. "Do you need the litter box?"

"Gracious no, the shop's got duplicates of everything. Haven't you been in yet?"

I admitted I hadn't had the opportunity. "Things have been kind of hectic lately."

"Oh, you owe yourself a visit. Heather has the most remarkable stock in her inventory."

"I don't doubt that for a minute."

As we split and went in different directions, Esmeralda

looked back at me, almost as if to say, "so this is how it's going to be." I offered a shrug and a wave. If she was upset about my informal farewell, I couldn't tell. But then I'd never been able to decipher the motives of any cat I'd known in my entire life.

CRAGG, THE ATTORNEY from upstairs, was in The Crocked Pot when I stopped in to grab a cup of coffee from Millie before heading over to the candle shop.

Cragg said grimly, "Harrison, I'd like a word with you."

"I need to get to my shop," I said as I gratefully took the cup Millie offered. She'd already learned my preferences and catered to them without being asked. It felt good being one of her regulars.

"I'll make it brief," he said, "but it is important."

Blast it all, I couldn't avoid the man, I was his landlord. "What can I do for you?" I asked as politely as I could manage, taking a sip of my coffee.

"I want to apologize for the way I acted before. I can be too aggressive for my own good sometimes, I realize that about myself. I shouldn't have pushed you like I did."

"No blood, no foul," I said. "I'm just sorry I couldn't help you."

"I'd like to do more as a way of apologizing," he said. "Let me think. Is there any legal representation I can handle for you?"

"Nobody's suing me that I know of," I said, trying to take some of the somber tone out of the conversation. "At least not yet."

He thought a moment, then said, "I know, I can draft your new will for you. Now that you're a man of some substance, you'll want to make certain things are taken care of if something should happen to you. I'd be honored to tender my services free of charge."

"I appreciate the offer, but to be honest with you, I don't know who I'd leave my things to. I'm the last Black left, at least from my particular branch of the family tree."

The attorney nodded. "If you should change your mind, I'd be delighted to help. The offer has no expiration date."

I offered my hand. "I appreciate the gesture."

He nodded and left as I added a little more cream to my coffee.

As I did, I looked up to see Millie smiling at me. "What's so amusing?" I asked.

"I feel like the Red Queen. I've seen two things today I never thought possible, and it's not even 9 AM yet."

"Okay, I'll bite. What are they?"

"A lawyer offering something for free, and a lunatic turning him down."

I grinned at her. "You never know, I might just need him if anybody ever sues me."

"Let's hope it doesn't come to that. I hear you're cat-sitting," she added as I was nearly to the door.

"Mrs. Quimby came by, I take it."

She laughed. "Come on, Harrison, you're spoiling my reputation as a psychic."

I said, "I won't tell a soul," as I left to open At Wick's End.

To my surprise, Eve was already there, a good hour before we were due to open.

Now what in the world was she up to?

I UNLOCKED THE door, intent on seeing what Eve was doing, when I heard the chime go off above my head. In all honesty, I'd forgotten all about it when I'd decided to slip inside.

Eve looked up at the sound, and was flustered a moment before she could speak.

"Good morning, Harrison," she said.

"You're in awfully early," I replied, trying to keep my voice casual. "Are you trying to show me up?"

She frowned slightly, then said, "I wanted to check on our inventories so I could order before we opened. I hope you don't mind."

"No, it's a great idea. In fact, I'll give you a hand. I made a preliminary list yesterday."

"It's not necessary," she said, a little more forcefully than was required. "I'm nearly finished, and I'm sure your list will just duplicate parts of mine. I can handle this myself."

"I insist. I've got to learn how to run my own candle shop."

She started to cloud up, and I quickly added, "If I'm ever going to be able to operate this place without calling you every two minutes, I need to learn how to do everything myself."

I walked back to the storage room before she could stop me and found a dozen boxes on the floor, all moved off the top shelves.

"It looks like a hurricane went through here."

Eve said, "That's another reason I came in early. Items are always falling behind the boxes. We find them later, after we've ordered duplicates we don't need. Belle and I started pulling the top inventories once a month to make sure we weren't missing anything."

I shook my head. "There's got to be a better way to do inventory than that."

"I'm just an employee," she said with a slight nod. "It's your store."

"I'll look into it," I said, making the hundredth mental note since I'd taken over the shop. "In the meantime, let me give you a hand getting this back into some kind of order."

We had things straightened out again soon enough, with everything back in its rightful place. There were three packs of wicks, one expensive rubber mold, a few scraps of paper and a handful of votive candle forms lodged behind the boxes.

"This won't take long to place, it's hardly big enough for you to bother with," Eve said as she studied the list.

"I'd still like to do it myself, if you don't mind. The quicker I learn, the better off I'll be."

She handed me the list and said, "You're welcome to it."

"Hey, I could use a walk-through first," I said, sorry I'd offended her yet again. "I don't even know who to call."

"I'm sure you'll have no problem at all, there's a list of our vendors by the telephone. Now if you'll excuse me, I have other work to do before we open."

As Eve started straightening the shelves out front, I stared after her. Most likely Belle had let her place the orders herself, but if I was going to get a handle on running the business, I had to know how to do everything in the store. I probably should have handled it more diplomatically, but I couldn't do anything about that at the moment. When things settled down, I'd try to make things right with Eve.

I dialed the number of our supplier and was waiting for someone to pick up when there was a knock at the office door. Good, it appeared that Eve had reconsidered and had decided to give me a hand.

Pearly stuck his head in and said, "We need to talk, Harrison."

"I'm kind of busy right now, Pearly."

"I can see that, but it would still be in your best interests to make that call later."

I hung up the phone and asked, "What's up?"

"Harrison, you don't know me all that well, but I'm not one to overreact to situations. Still, there's something going on here that requires your attention." He paused a moment, then added, "I'm beginning to suspect this new tenant Markum is up to something."

"What makes you think that?" I asked, suddenly forgetting all about the supply order.

"Last night I was upstairs adding a new dead-bolt lock to Cragg's office when I saw the oddest thing. Markum didn't notice me, I was on the inside of Cragg's office with the door cracked. He walked up the stairs with a bag slung over one shoulder, and from the strain on his face, I'll wager there was a heavy load in that duffel."

"He's into salvage, Pearly. It could have been anything."

"I might concur, if that were all. However, I needed a different tool from my truck for the installation, and as I walked by his office I heard him on the telephone." Pearly colored slightly. "Now I wasn't eavesdropping, but he'd neglected to close his door, and the man's voice does have a way of carrying."

"What did you hear?" I asked, in spite of the invasion of privacy. If Markum had anything to do with Belle's death, I wanted to know about it. Courtesies, even legalities, didn't bother me much if they stood in the way of me finding the truth.

"There was quite a bit of shouting; I caught references to payments being late, and then there were some questions about glass for sale."

"Glass?" That got my attention. "What else did he say about that?"

"Just that some of it had to be cut first. I assumed that part had something to do with a broken window, but the rest of the argument was quite forceful."

"I'll talk to him tonight," I promised.

"Fair enough, that would ease my mind." Pearly paused, then added, "I'm as level a man as you'll most likely find, Harrison, but there's something odd in the air around River's Edge lately, and I can't for the life of me figure out what it is."

It was murder, I thought, but I kept it to myself. Pearly was absolutely one of my least likely suspects in the search for my great-aunt's killer, but I couldn't let the fact that I liked him impede my judgment. I liked just about everyone at River's Edge, with the possible exception of Gary Cragg. Markum seemed like a straightforward fellow with a good disposition, but that didn't exclude him either. It would be hard to imagine Millie or Heather or Eve doing anything to Belle, but that didn't take them off my list. Until I could prove otherwise, every last one of them was a legitimate suspect.

The only problem was that my list kept growing with suspects as I added new people, but I never managed to eliminate anyone. If I couldn't discover who was involved in Belle's death, maybe I could start from the other end and try to eliminate some of the suspects I had.

It was bound to be better than my current approach.

By nightfall I hoped to speak with Markum about that glass. I'd read enough mysteries to know that it was also a term used as slang for diamonds, and I had a sneaking suspicion I knew what that might be connected with.

I STILL HAD a little time before we opened the candle shop, so I told Eve I'd be back before we opened and returned to The Crocked Pot. Millie was just finishing up with a customer when I decided it was time to try to strike her off my list.

"What's the matter, Harrison, did you forget something?"

"Do you have a second?" I asked her.

"For you? I've got all the time in the world." As Millie said it, she polished the top of the counter with her rag.

"If you don't mind, I'd like to ask you a question."

Her ever-present smile dimmed as she nodded. "Okay by me. Fire away."

"Were you around River's Edge the night Belle died?"

She looked shocked by the question. "What an odd question. Why do you want to know that?"

"Honestly? I was hoping maybe you noticed something, or saw someone hanging around who shouldn't have been here that night." If she gave me a positive answer, I'd know whether Millie had been there herself without asking her for an alibi directly.

Millie pondered a moment, then said, "I know, I was with George at the baseball game. He's a fanatic for the Ridge Runners, and it was their first home playoff game. Their last one too, I might add, the dear boys didn't do well."

So Millie was out with a crowd of three thousand other folks at our local single A baseball team's game.

I said, "Was there anyone in Belle's life most folks around here wouldn't have known about?"

Millie shook her head, then said, "I don't think so."

"If you come up with any names outside of River's Edge, let me know, okay?"

"I'll do it."

"Thanks." If I did as Pearly had suggested and went with my gut, Millie had to be ruled out as a suspect. It would be easy enough to check to see if she'd really been to the game, but I wasn't about to do it unless she gave me the slightest reason to suspect her.

It was time for me to get to work. I headed back to the candle shop and dove into the day, even venturing out from behind the cash register now and then to actually help a few customers myself. Eve was never more than a few steps away, but she showed remarkable restraint by letting me handle things myself.

By that afternoon, I was starting to get the hang of running At Wick's End. We were nearly ready to close for the day when Eve asked, "Did they say when our order would ship?"

"Order?" I asked as I went through the stack of credit card receipts.

"Don't tell me you've forgotten already. I'm talking about the order you placed for the store this morning. You did call it in, didn't you?"

"Blast it all, I got distracted. I'll go do it right now."

Eve looked at the clock and said, "They're already closed for the day." She looked pointedly at me as she added, "That's because they open so early in the morning, before the stores get busy and don't have time to call."

"I'll phone them first thing tomorrow," I said, feeling my face burn.

Eve didn't answer, and I knew I'd earned her disapproval yet again. That was just too bad. I was about to throw another log on the fire.

When I asked Eve where she'd been the night Belle died, giving the same reason I had to Millie, she said, "I was home alone. How terrible that Belle had to die that way, without another soul around her."

That was exactly what I was trying to find out. "Did you get any calls or visitors that night?"

Eve shook her head. "My evenings are solitary, Harrison. Honestly, that's the way I like it after dealing with our customers all day. There are times when I turn the telephone ringer off and ignore my doorbell."

So far nobody was willing to admit they'd been within ten miles of River's Edge, but I still didn't believe Belle fell off that ladder on her own.

Eve and I were nearly ready to lock up for the night when Mrs. Jorgenson came in. She looked around the empty store, then said, "Mr. Black, would you mind walking me out to my car? There's something I'd like to discuss with you."

"Was there a problem with your bill?" I asked, worried that I had indeed overcharged her for the lessons. Eve looked like she was going to pass out.

"No, it's nothing like that. This is a personal matter."

Eve looked quizzically at me, but I just shrugged. "Let's go."

Once we were outside, Mrs. Jorgenson said, "I debated telling you this, but there's something I feel you need to know. I received a rather quizzical call about you this afternoon."

"What? About me?"

"Whoever was on the other end of the line refused to identify themself, and the voice was a whisper. I couldn't even tell if it was a man or a woman."

"And you say my name was mentioned?" What was going on here?

"Oh yes. Apparently someone has a grudge against you. They implied that it would be unhealthy for me to continue with our private lessons."

"I don't know what to say." I was nearly speechless by the revelation.

She looked sternly at me, then said, "My dear man, you

have no need to worry that an idle threat will keep me away from your candle shop. I don't respond to pressure, I never have. I told them so quite emphatically." She grinned slightly at the thought, then added, "I did think you should know though."

"Thanks, I appreciate that."

As I watched her drive away, I tried to figure out who in the world would try to submarine me like that. Was there a competitor out there who begrudged my chance at Mrs. Jorgenson? Or was it something more ominous? There couldn't be anything random about the call, since my name was mentioned specifically. I considered discussing it with Eve, but since there was nothing either one of us could do about it, I decided to keep it to myself, at least for the moment.

Twelve

AFTER I closed the candle shop, I headed straight to the bank with our day's deposit. That was one lesson I had learned without danger of repeating. I got there before they closed since this was one of the rare nights we shut the doors before dark, and decided to take it inside myself.

A bright-eyed young lady took the bag, made quick work of checking my amounts, then handed a slip to me. "Is that all, sir?"

I suddenly remembered my own check, still folded up in my wallet. "I'd like to cash this too."

It felt good having money in my pocket again as I put the crisp new bills in my wallet. My meager savings were nearly depleted. I promised myself to move my checking account to the new bank, since it would be so much more convenient doing all my business at one place.

After I finished at the bank, I found a grocery store along the way back to River's Edge and decided to go on a little shopping spree. Forty minutes later, I'd put a noticeable dent in my take home pay, but my larder would be well-stocked for the next few weeks.

I found Mrs. Quimby waiting impatiently for me at my door when I got back, Esmeralda squirming in her hands. "Harrison, did you forget about your star boarder?"

Blast and nonsense, it had slipped my mind completely that I was still cat-sitting, even after I picked up a toy for Esme while I was out shopping. "I'm so sorry. I got hung up at the grocery store," I said as I put my bags down and retrieved my key.

Mrs. Quimby sniffed at the air and said, "I don't mind, but the princess is quite upset. She hates to wait for anything."

I didn't doubt that. Esmeralda seemed to be the type of cat who considered anything short of complete and utter devotion an unacceptable outrage.

"She'll have to get over it," I said as I opened the door. "My schedule's not quite as set as Heather's is."

Esme shot through and disappeared inside before I could even get my key back out of the lock.

"You two have a fun evening together," she said quickly as she walked away.

"Thanks. Sorry again about the delay."

After I put away my groceries, I went in search of my boarder. "Esme. Come here, Esmeralda."

I should have realized it was the height of futility calling a cat. While a dog would most likely come running at the sound of its name, that cat was probably holed up somewhere laughing at me. Then I remembered one of Janie's tricks. I pulled out the can opener and opened one of Esmeralda's dinner tins.

After a minute, she poked her head around the corner to see what I was up to as I arranged the meal tastefully in her bowl, and as she began to eat, it was obvious that we were friends again.

After making myself a sandwich and letting Esme finish her meal, I said, "Hey, I almost forgot. I got you something." I retrieved a plush mouse toy I'd picked up at the grocery store and put it on the floor in front of her. If a cat could sneer, this one was doing it. I tried to make the mouse dance on the string, hoping to get some action out of her that way, but by the way Esme was looking at me, it was clear she thought I was insane.

I was beginning to concur with her opinion by the time I gave up.

I cleaned up the dishes, lit Belle's candle and settled onto the couch to read. That's when I noticed Esmeralda, playing not with the mouse, but with the packing it had come in, batting it back and forth from one paw to another.

It was all I could do to keep a groan from escaping my lips. The cat waited until I was settled in, then hopped up onto my lap and eased in for the evening. I suddenly remembered my earlier plan to confront Markum.

"Up you go," I said as I dislodged an indignant cat.

I added, "I'll be back before you know I'm gone. Why don't you play with your new friend Mr. Packing while I'm out?" Why was I explaining all this to a cat?

Esmeralda told me exactly what she thought of my suggestion by turning and showing me her tail as she vanished into the bedroom.

Maybe she'd understood me after all.

WONDER OF WONDERS, Markum was in his office when I knocked on the door.

"Harrison, it looks like you're keeping my hours now," he said in his booming voice.

I glanced at my watch and saw that it was nearly ten o'clock. "Being a landlord is turning out to be a full-time job. I hope you didn't lose anything in the lockers when they were vandalized."

He shook his head as he led me back to his office. "No sir, I keep everything I need locked up in here." The walls of the small room were covered with travel posters of exotic beaches, snowcapped mountain ranges and lush dense forests, and I realized that whichever way he swiveled in his chair, Markum would have a perfect view of the great outdoors.

He noticed my wandering gaze. "What can I say, I'm a pushover for exotic spots. Do you like to travel, Harrison?"

"I've never really been able to afford it," I admitted. "At least not on the scale we're talking about here."

"Well, you're a man of money now. This building's got to be worth a mint, sitting on the river like it is. Belle must have been slipping to rent a spot to me."

"Why is that?" I asked.

"I'm not exactly what you'd call a typical tenant, don't you think I know that? My hours are odd, to say the least, and I've got my fingers in a dozen different pies at any one time. What I do isn't exactly something that I could put in a brochure, either."

"You're in salvaging and recovery, you said. That must be exciting, but what exactly does it mean? Do you spend a lot of time diving?"

"There are more things in this world to be salvaged than shipwrecks, though I've gone after more than a couple of those in my day."

I glanced toward the room's only closet and saw a safe partially through the open door.

Markum followed my glance and nudged the door closed with his foot. "You can't be too careful, this day and age."

The ringing of the telephone interrupted him, and he said, "Excuse me, I've got to take this call. I've been waiting for it all day and half the night."

He took the portable phone out of his office into the hallway, pacing as he spoke. Markum's voice was animated; there was no doubt about that. I could well imagine it echoing off the empty hallways if his door happened to be open.

While he was gone, I stood and flipped around an open notebook on his desktop.

I don't know what I was hoping to find; a full confession maybe, or better yet, plans to knock off another jewelry store.

Instead, I found numbers in no apparent sequence scrawled on the pad, surrounded by doodles of girls in hula attire. If Markum ever decided to give up his salvage business, he might be able to freelance as a cartoonist.

I heard his voice grow louder and spun the notebook back to facing the chair again. The only problem was that in my nervousness, I'd spun it a little too hard and it was pointed right back at me again like an accusing finger. His voice was nearly at the door when I nudged it again, this time much gentler, and it slowly slid back into place as I heard Markum say behind me, "Just do it and stop bellyaching."

"Sorry," he said as he took his position back behind the desk again. "I've got a sub who's getting cold feet."

"A sub?"

"Subcontractor. I can't do everything, not and do a thorough job of it, so I hire a little extra help when I need it. That particular fellow found he doesn't have what it takes a little too late after promising me he did."

"So what's going to happen to him?"

Markum smiled, reading the seriousness in my voice. "If he doesn't play ball, I'll deal with him in my own way. So Harrison, is this a social visit, or did you have something on your mind?"

"It's about Belle," I said. "I understand the two of you had a fight a few weeks ago."

"Who's been feeding you that crock of nonsense?"

I said, "I'd rather not say, but it did concern me." I wasn't about to admit that Millie had told me about it.

Markum leaned back in his chair, his head nearly touching the back wall. "Harrison, I'm an animated fellow. I like to bellow, it's a part of my nature. The only thing I can figure is someone overheard your great-aunt and me having a lively discussion, and they mistook it for an argument. She was a fine lady, one the world will miss. I know I certainly will. We never had anything close to what I'd call an argument during the short time we knew each other."

"Can I ask you something?" I said.

"You can ask, but I won't promise you an answer, especially if it concerns my business. There's something you need to understand, and pass on to your little informant.

My business is just that, my business. Tell that tattletale of yours if they have a problem with me, they need to face me directly. Now what was your question?"

I took a deep breath, then said, "I was wondering if you could tell me where you were and what you were doing the night Belle died."

Markum said steadily, "What are you up to?"

"Tell me or don't, it's your business. If you liked her as much as you said you did, why wouldn't you then?"

"Easy, I didn't mean to offend you. It just sounds like you're looking for alibis. I happened to be out of town when it happened, working the Outer Banks studying something that didn't pan out. Harrison, as much as I'd love to hang around here and chat, I'm having second thoughts about that sub of mine. Maybe I'd better pay him a visit in person. I can be quite persuasive when I need to be."

"I'll bet," I said as I followed him out of his office. I noticed he had three shiny new locks on his door as he secured each one in turn.

He smiled. "Like I said, you can't be too careful these days. I had these installed right after you had your locks changed. See you around, Harrison."

"I'll be here," I said.

"And where else could you possibly go, with this new mistress of yours?" Before I could say anything, his arm swept around me. "I imagine River's Edge is quite a demanding lady."

THE SECOND I got back to the apartment, it was obvious Esmeralda hadn't been pleased with my departure. Somehow she'd managed to unroll every paper towel from the dispenser in the kitchen. There was a trail of it throughout the apartment. Not only that, but she'd discovered the toilet paper holder as well. She had saved that for the bedroom. I found the cat perched on my pillow, partially wrapped in the paper herself. There was a stern look on her face, as if she were daring me to say a word.

I wanted to laugh, but Janie had taught me early on that cats didn't have much of a sense of humor, especially about themselves, so I cleaned up the mess and figured we were even for my deserting her. By the time I had the kitchen cleaned up, she'd managed to extricate herself from her swathing.

As I collected the fallen rolls, my mind kept drifting back to my conversation with the salvage man. Markum was someone so different from what I was used to, it was difficult to gauge the man and his reactions. It was almost as if he was shielded by his nature, giving a shining smile to the world while calculating the odds and angles just beneath it.

After some order was restored to the apartment, I said loudly, "Okay, you made your point. You don't like being left alone. I'm going to read in the other room now, and you're welcome to join me." Blast it all if that cat didn't hop up from the bed and follow me into the living room.

A part of me was going to be happy when Heather returned, but another part realized that Esmeralda was growing on me, that I might actually miss her when she was gone.

Not that I would ever have admitted it to anyone else. Especially to the cat.

I WOKE UP to the sounds of mewing the next morning. It appeared that my roommate was hungry, and wasn't the least bit reluctant to share that news with me. Heather hadn't told me anything about the frequency of Esmeralda's diet, but I couldn't take that pitiful sound, so I opened another can for her.

"It looks like this is going to be our last day together, Esme," I said as we both ate our breakfasts.

The cat studied me a moment before going back to her food.

"I just wanted to say you're welcome any time. As long as you can resist the rolls of paper around here."

There was a knock at the door, and I was surprised to find Heather there.

"You're back early," I said as I led her into the apartment.

"Mom's much better. I went home with her last night, but she was ready to be on her own, so I was told in no uncertain terms that it was time for me to leave."

"Ouch," I said. "That had to hurt."

"Not really, it just meant that she was feeling better. Hey, sweetheart, did you forget all about me?" Heather said to her cat.

Esme looked at her, seemed to think about it a moment, then walked casually toward her owner.

Heather scooped her up, laughing. "I missed you too, you rascal. I see you've duped Harrison into overfeeding you."

"Sorry," I said. "I didn't know her schedule."

Heather laughed. "Don't worry, she's a great con artist. I'll be back a little later for her things, if that's all right with you. I want to open early and check on the store."

"Tell you what. I'll bring everything to At Wick's End and you can get it there." I considered stroking Esme's head, then thought better of it. In a formal tone, I said, "It was a pleasure rooming with you, Dame Esmeralda."

Heather smiled. "I'm glad you two got along."

"We had our moments, but I believe we ultimately managed to forge a bond of trust."

"Harrison, you are too funny. Thanks again."

As Heather carried her cat away, I could swear that rascal swished her tail at me before the door closed.

I got ready to go downstairs, amazed by how empty the apartment felt without Esmeralda's presence.

I OPENED AT Wick's End with no sign of Eve in sight. As the minutes ticked down to the opening hour, my sense of panic grew stronger and stronger. Had something driven her off again? The least she could have done was call me. I got everything ready for opening, half-expecting her to show up at any time, but when I finally unlocked the door to officially start the business day, I was completely alone.

"Deep breaths, Harrison, you can handle this," I told myself as I waited for my first customer.

A young woman with the wildest tangled hair I'd ever seen in my life came in two minutes after I opened.

"Where's Eve?" she said before I could offer a "good morning" to her.

"She's running late," I said, hoping that was true. "Can I help you?"

"You're new here, aren't you? If Eve's not available, Belle will do."

I pursed my lips, then said solemnly, "I'm sorry to be the one to tell you this, but Belle's gone."

"Where did she go?" the woman asked, a slight annoyance in her voice. "She didn't quit her own store, did she?"

There really wasn't any delicate way to put it. "Belle died a few days ago."

The words hung between us for what felt like days before she said somberly, "I'm so sorry to hear that." She paused, then added, "Well, how about you? Do you know anything about molds?"

"A bit," I admitted.

"My candles keep sticking, and I can't for the life of me figure out what I'm doing wrong. I just started this crazy hobby and it's already driving me insane."

I led her to the section with waxes and releases. "You have a couple of options," I said. "You can add stearin, it causes the wax to shrink some as it hardens. Then there's mold release. You coat your mold with it before you make your pour."

She studied me, then said, "I'd say you know more than a little bit about all this."

"What can I say, I'm a quick study. So which will it be?"

"Tell you what, give me some of each. And I'll take another ten pounds of wax and a packet of wicks while you're at it. I don't get into town all that much."

After I rang up her order and bagged the supplies, the

woman shot a hand across the register to me. "I'm Emmaline Hannah. Listen, I'm really sorry about Belle. I only met her once, but I thought she had a sweet spirit. So you're running things now."

"I am. My name's Harrison Black."

She gave me a bright smile, then said, "Well Harrison Black, it's good to meet you. I'd love to stand around and chat half the morning away, but there are things to do, places to go, and folks to pester."

After she was gone, I had to smile myself. At Wick's End certainly had its share of eccentric customers. Somehow it made me feel right at home.

Thirteen

JUST as I began to give up all hope of ever seeing Eve again, she walked in the door a little after 1 PM.

"You could have called," I said as she hung up her coat.

"Why on earth would I want to do that?" she said.

"We open at 9:00 AM," I replied a little frostily.

"But I don't come in until one today. I thought that was what you wanted. Didn't you look at the schedule, Harrison?"

"I didn't know we had one," I said as I put a few extra bags under the counter. I'd had a busy morning, selling quite a bit of small-priced stock, a dollar here and there that still managed to add up to a respectable total.

She said, "I suppose I understand your pique. The schedule's on the back of the office door."

I walked back, with Eve on my heels. Once we were inside, I closed the door, and sure enough, there was a schedule in Belle's crisp handwriting.

"I'm sorry, you're right, but I thought you weren't coming in at all today." I added softly, "You promised me you'd work full-time this week."

"I didn't assume that meant I had to be here whenever you were. On the evenings I teach classes here, I never come in until one. I'm going to have quite a bit of overtime as it is." Eve shook her head. "Harrison, given my action Sunday I can't hold it against you, but you should know that I would never miss a shift, at least not without calling you first."

"I should have figured it out on my own. So what's the class about this evening?"

"Actually, you might consider sitting in. I'm teaching four students how to pour candles. It should help you get a feel for what we do in our general classes."

"It sounds great. Do you mind covering for me while I go get something to eat? I'm starving."

"That's why I'm here. Take your time at lunch. I've got the store under control."

I walked outside and thought about getting a slice of pizza and a Coke at A Slice of Heaven, but I decided to make a sandwich upstairs and eat it on the steps of River's Edge. I loved the convenience of having Millie right there and the pizza parlor not much farther away, but if I bought my breakfast and lunch from other people every day, I'd end up losing money every week, certainly spending more than I could afford.

I slapped a sandwich together, walked downstairs and back out into the lovely weather. A breeze had kicked up in the short time I'd been upstairs, and I found myself wishing for a light jacket.

My friends the ducks were back when I returned to the spot where Heather and I had picnicked, and I was ready for them. I'd packed an extra piece of bread just for them, and they gobbled it down with great delight. The simple meal was enhanced by the day, as I found myself sliding happily into the new life Belle had chosen for me. I felt guilty not pursuing my suspicions surrounding her death more vigorously, but if anyone in the world would understand how much work it was to run At Wick's End, it would have been Belle. Still, I promised myself as soon as

I got a little breathing room, I'd do a little more digging and find out what had really happened to her.

THE REST OF the afternoon raced past, and after another quick bite upstairs during the half hour we were closed between regular hours and the scheduled evening class, it was time to get started. I helped Eve lay out the supplies we'd need, adding an extra of each at another bench so I could follow along myself. We had hot plate burners at each station, double-boilers, chunks of wax, wicks, and an array of dye blocks and bottled concentrated scents.

Eve surveyed my work, then said, "We need some ice from the freezer, but wait a while before you get that." She also grabbed some odd chunks of colored wax, along with baskets filled with seashells and pretty rocks.

"What are these for," I asked as I ran my hand through the basket at my table.

"You'll see."

There was a knock on the front door, and Eve glanced at the clock. "Right on time. Would you let them in, Harrison?"

I nodded and headed to the front of the store. A group of four women spanning the generations were waiting for me, from eight years old to eighty. They appeared to run the gamut from great-granddaughter to the grand matriarch herself.

The grandmother asked, "Are we early? We couldn't wait to get started."

I bent just short of a royal bow. "Come in, ladies. I'm Harrison Black."

The eldest in the group said, "I was under the impression a woman named Eve would be our instructor this evening."

"I'm observing tonight, if you don't mind," I said as I locked up behind them. The last thing we wanted were customers wandering in during the class. Besides, I'd been on my feet all day. The idea of sitting at one of the benches instead of waiting on other folks was pretty appealing.

"We'd be delighted to have you," another of the women said, no doubt the youngest girl's mother. "Isn't that right, Grandma?"

"Certainly. The more the merrier."

The one who had acquiesced said, "This is her birthday, and she wanted to make candles."

I said, "My most hearty congratulations, ma'am. Happy birthday."

"It certainly has been so far," she said with a twinkle of light in her eyes.

I led them back to the benches, and Eve took over with the practiced ease of someone who had taught the class dozens of times before. It was amazing watching her work with each of the ladies, making them feel special as we all created our own candles. I learned a great deal watching her, and not just about working with wax. Eve called each woman by her correct name from the beginning, an ability I was going to have to cultivate. I was horrible with names, forgetting them at the most embarrassing moments.

We were nearing the time to pour when Eve held up one of the baskets of shells and polished stones. "These make quite a nice accent when they are floated in your candle. You can also use chunks of colored waxes," she said as she pointed them out. "You can even use ice. They all make lovely candles." Eve passed around a series of poured candles she'd already made to the women, and I collected them as they finished studying the varied effects. I'd seen candles with things embedded in them before, but honestly, I'd never thought about how they'd gotten there.

Eve asked, "Harrison, would you get the ice please?"

I went back to the office and opened the tiny freezer of our small refrigerator, removing enough cubes of ice to make a small pitcher of tea.

After we prepared our candle molds and individually melted waxes with all the scents and colors we wanted, it was time to pour. I half-expected Eve to just cut everyone loose, but she insisted on one pour at a time. "Remember, this wax is approaching two hundred degrees. It will burn you if it touches your skin, so be careful." This sobered the ladies somewhat, and it nearly scared the little girl to death.

Eve must have seen the fright in her eyes. "Kathy, would you like to go first? Don't worry, I'll be right beside you. You'll do fine."

The little girl looked unsure, and her mother was about to intervene when Eve added, "In fact, why don't I help you pour? There's a knack to getting it just right."

"That would be great," the little girl said, obviously relieved to have the burden lifted from her.

Eve picked the pitcher up with an oven mitt on her hand, had Kathy put one on herself, then wiped off the accumulated moisture from the side of the pitcher before the two of them managed to get nearly all of the wax into the mold.

The older women applauded the effort, and I clapped right along beside them as the task was completed.

"Now who wants to go next?" Eve said.

When it was finally my turn, I put a single shell into the bottom of the mold, along with one stone. Eve said, "Harrison, your items are going to be swallowed up by the wax this way. Unless you're trying to hide them, you need to add more, and space them around the perimeter of the candle so they'll show through."

Kathy chuckled softly at the gentle scolding and I shared a wink and a smile with her as I put more baubles into the bottom of the mold and arranged them in a better order.

"How's that?" I asked.

"Excellent." She glanced into my brightly blue-toned wax and said, "We can dilute that somewhat with more wax. It's rather strong."

"I wanted something bold," I said.

"It's your candle," she said, so I made my pour.

"Now what happens?" Kathy's mother asked. "Can we take them with us tonight?"

"Harrison and I still need to add a little more to each

after the wax settles, then they need a day to cool completely. If someone wishes to come by at closing tomorrow, they will be ready. Thanks again for coming, and Happy Birthday."

"That was absolutely delightful," the matriarch said. "Now Kathy," she said, taking her great-granddaughter's hand, "why don't we go back home and have a touch more cake."

"Mother, you're spoiling her," Kathy's mother said.

"That's my job."

"And how well you do it. You two will have to share a piece, and it's going to have to be a little one at that. Kathy, you've already had too much as it is."

The two eldest ladies winked at each other, and I had a sneaky suspicion Kathy was going to be getting a double serving, whether Mom knew about it or not. As I locked up after them, it made me realize just how alone I was in the world. Here was a family of four generations, getting along like the best of friends, while I was the last twig of the last branch of my family tree.

It made me miss Belle even more.

AFTER EVE AND I topped off the candles with the reheated wax, it was time to close the place up for the night.

"So I'll see you in the morning?" I asked as we walked out of the store.

"Bright and early. Sorry for the confusion today, Harrison, I really did think you knew."

"Not a problem. I appreciate the lesson tonight. It was great fun."

"I had good students," she said. "Besides, I assumed you could use the practice before Mrs. Jorgenson comes back in."

"If we pour candles then," I said. "Who knows what she'll decide come Monday."

"I doubt she'll be content to keep rolling candles, not when there are so many other techniques in candlemaking.

She wants to learn it all, so you'll need to be ready for her. That makes her the perfect student in my mind."

"It doesn't hurt that she's able to pay our fees either, does it?"

"As you said, we do have to make a profit," Eve replied, a statement I heartily endorsed.

I NEVER COULD have imagined how much companionship Esmeralda offered during her brief stay with me until she was gone. Belle's apartment was lonelier than it had ever been without the weight of Esme on my lap as I read. Even Dame Agatha had trouble holding my attention, and I knew the problem lay with the reader, not the author.

I finally put the book down and decided what I needed was something to take my mind off Esmeralda's absence. When I'd been cleaning out Belle's closet, I'd noticed a set of odd U-shaped iron bars embedded in the wall leading to a scuttle of some sort in the ceiling. Perhaps there was an attic up there. I'd been curious about it, but hadn't had the time to do much exploring until now.

I climbed the steps and found a dead bolt hidden within the top that secured the cover firmly. Not knowing if it would even open, I threw the bolt and pushed, expecting great resistance.

The cover nearly flew out of my hands.

Somebody had used the scuttle frequently enough to want to keep the hinges well-lubricated. I couldn't imagine Belle climbing that iron ladder, but the old gal had fooled me more than once over the past week. Eve had told me about Belle's recent fear of heights, but I knew firsthand that she hadn't always felt that way. She'd been a fixture in every tree house I'd ever built, prodding my imagination with stories of pirate ships and great castles as we swayed high above the ground.

When I looked up, I found myself staring at the clouds of the evening sky. I wasn't about to go traipsing around on the roof without some kind of light to guide me, but my curiosity wouldn't allow me to wait till morning to check it out. There wasn't a flashlight anywhere in sight, but I did see Belle's candle on the table and the matches beside it. I grabbed those, then climbed up awkwardly with my added burden.

It was amazing, standing up on that roof as the night crept in. Micah's Ridge was laid out below me in the distance as twilight came. There was something about the darkness that enhanced the town's beauty, hiding the bad and highlighting the good until the last whispers of light finally faded away.

Belle had a lawn chair set up under an umbrella stand anchored beside it. The umbrella was chained to the stand, lying on the roof next to it. I couldn't imagine Belle up there, but who else would even know about the scuttle that ran through her closet, unless there was another opening somewhere else on the roof. I lit the candle, watched the flame flicker then take hold as I cupped one hand around the wick to block the breeze that was still kicking around. It was amazing how much illumination the candle put out, or perhaps my eyes were growing used to the reduced light. I walked all over the roof with great confidence, being careful to stay away from the edge.

There was no other access to the roof, at least none that I could see. So Belle had found a private hideaway she hadn't had to share with anyone else in the world. I decided to continue the tradition. It could surely come in handy, having a place to go where no one else could find me.

I was ready to go back inside when I heard a clattering on the ground below in back of River's Edge. It was the unmistakable sound of steel hitting pavement, and I couldn't help but wonder who was out this late, and what they were up to. I crept carefully to the edge and was startled to see a dark form fleeing from the direction of my old Dodge truck, the vehicle I'd virtually abandoned since getting Belle's newer and nicer Ford.

Why would someone try to steal my old truck when a newer, nicer one was six feet away from it? I wished I had a spotlight instead of the candle in my hand so I could see who was fleeing into the night. I had no doubt they couldn't see me, even if they looked up. The lip on the roof was enough to shield all but the brightest light. I was still peering after the retreating figure when a gust of wind came up. I'd forgotten to shield the candle and found myself blind in the sudden absence of light. One wrong step and I knew I could plummet to the ground below.

Fourteen

I groped in my pockets for the matches, but they must have fallen out sometime during my exploration of the roof. Now what was I going to do?

I really had no choice. I forced myself to stand there in the shivering darkness until I got my night vision, at least enough to get safely back to the scuttle. As I waited for my eyes to adjust to the darkness, the breeze grew stronger and stronger, and I felt the gusts tugging at me, pushing me with whispering fingers toward the edge.

Finally, after what seemed like an eternity, I could make out shapes and definitions on the roof around me. I turned and walked slowly back toward the opening, and when I got close enough, I could make out the raised edges of the scuttle. I'd closed the hatch when I'd exited, and I was relieved when it opened easily at my touch.

I hurried down the steps and rushed downstairs, but whoever had been there was now long gone.

But why would anyone want something with my old truck? I was going to have to wait until morning before I could answer that question. There was not a thing in the world I could do about it until then.

I CALLED MY mechanic and friend Wayne Darrell the first thing the next morning. "Hey, buddy, I need a favor."

"You and everybody else. When are we going to play tennis again? I'm beginning to forget which end of the racket to hold."

"No time soon. I don't know if you've heard, but my great-aunt died."

Wayne's teasing ended abruptly. "I'm sorry. Is there anything I can do?"

"No, she didn't want a service or anything, but I've taken over her store. It's a candle shop," I said, waiting for a jab.

Wayne said, "Sounds good. It's got to be better than selling those junk computers. So what's up?"

"Listen, this is going to sound crazy, but I was up on the roof last night and I saw somebody messing with the Dodge."

Wayne laughed at that. "You mean they were trying to steal it? You could leave that thing running in front of a convenience store at midnight and nobody would take it. It's a wreck. Wait a second. What were you doing up on a roof at night? You feeling okay, buddy? You haven't been depressed lately, have you?"

"I wasn't going to jump, you nitwit, I was checking out the stars." I didn't want to admit that I'd been satisfying my curiosity, not being able to wait until morning light.

Wayne said, "It was overcast last night. You were snooping, weren't you?"

"I was exploring," I admitted. "That's entirely different."

Wayne said, "Okay, okay, you were exploring. When you say someone was messing with your truck, what exactly do you mean? Were they trying to get in the door?"

"I heard steel hitting the pavement, like some kind of heavy tool was dropped. I don't know, I've just got a bad feeling about this."

Wayne said abruptly, "Don't do anything till I get there. Don't even go near it, okay?"

"What do you think, somebody put a bomb under it?"

Wayne ignored my question and asked, "What kind of trouble have you gotten yourself into where you're worried about bombs? Come clean, Harrison."

I tried to laugh it off. "You know what? Forget about it. I'm probably just being paranoid."

"Hey, don't hang up," he said. "Tell me where you're at. I want to check it out before you go near it."

"I'm at a place called River's Edge. Do you know where it is?"

"Are you kidding me, I'm a huge fan of Millie's pumpkin doughnuts at The Crocked Pot. I remember seeing a candle shop over there too. Is that where you're at?"

"The name of the shop is At Wick's End."

"No, that doesn't sound right."

I said, "Believe me, that's the name. I've been working there every day for over a week."

He said, "Okay, okay. Listen, I want you to do what I ask, all joking aside. Go stand near your truck and wait for me, but don't touch it. Don't even breathe on it, Harrison, promise?"

"I think you're crazier than I am, but I won't do anything until you get here."

After we hung up, there was nothing I could do but go down by the truck and wait. Wayne showed up ten minutes later in his tow truck. As he got out, he studied the back of River's Edge and said, "Nice place. Is it all yours, or just the candle shop?"

It was pretty obvious he was kidding. "It's all mine, down to the last brick."

Wayne studied me for a second, then said, "So your ship finally came in. Sorry it had to happen that way."

I said, "You want to know the truth? The bank owns it, I don't. I've never been more in debt in my life."

Wayne said, "Welcome to my world." He looked at the Dodge, started to flick off a piece of peeling paint and then changed his mind. "I can't believe you're still driving this thing."

I pointed to the Ford. "I'm not. My great-aunt left me that. But not everybody knows that. In fact, the guy who's handling the will forgot to tell me about it."

"Okay, enough guessing about what's really going on here. Let's see what we've got." Wayne got down on the ground and wiggled under the truck. He spent less than two minutes under it before he crawled back out again.

I felt like an idiot. "Okay, I admit it. I've got an overactive imagination. Sorry to drag you over here like this for nothing."

There was no smile on Wayne's face. "It's a good thing you did. Somebody nicked your brake line, buddy. I'd say you've got yourself a real enemy after all."

So somebody really was after me. I suddenly realized that if I hadn't been out on the roof last night, I never would have known about the sabotage. Granted I didn't plan on driving the Dodge much, but the first time I did, I would have been in serious trouble.

Wayne said, "You want me to call the cops?"

"Yes. Maybe. No."

"Okay, you've given me a handful of possible answers. Now which one are we going with?"

I said, "Keep this to yourself, okay? I don't want to involve the police. They think I'm paranoid as it is."

"At least let me tow it in," Wayne said. "I can have it fixed in an hour."

I grabbed his arm and said, "If whoever did this thinks their little plan is still going to work, they won't try anything else, will they? Let's leave it alone for now."

"Harrison, I don't know what kind of game you're playing, but it doesn't sound like it's got many rules."

I said, "I think we're making them up as we go along. Listen, I'll buy you a beer when this is all over and let you know what happened."

"I'd rather have a can of tennis balls, with you on the other end of the court."

"I promise, just as soon as things slow down. Thanks again for coming out, Wayne."

He patted my shoulder. "Listen, if you need backup, day or night, call me, do you hear me?"

"I'll do it."

He got into his truck and drove away.

And I was left knowing that someone, for whatever reason, was trying to get rid of me. Once and for all.

I GRABBED A quick breakfast back upstairs at the apartment, then headed to At Wick's End.

I had a call to make.

Becka picked up on the third ring. "Hello," she said groggily.

"Sorry to wake you, but you asked me to call you."

The transformation was miraculous as she suddenly perked up. "Harrison. I was just about to get up. Thanks for calling."

"You're welcome. Listen, I was wondering if you could stop by the candle shop sometime this morning. There's something I'd really like to talk to you about."

"Really? Give me a hint. You know how I hate surprises." Her voice had taken on a playful tone that for some reason I had once found endearing.

"Sorry, you're going to have to wait. Can you make it sometime before ten?"

"Give me an hour and I'll be there."

That would be perfect. Eve wasn't scheduled to come in until twelve. "See you then."

After I hung up, I worked at straightening the shelves, putting items back in their original places. It was like a game of hide-and-seek with some of the customers, seeing just how far something could be abandoned away from its proper spot.

Miracle of miracles, Becka was earlier than her promised hour. She must have been more eager than I thought. She had pulled out all the stops, opting for a short skirt that showed off her legs, spiked heels that looked impossible to walk in, and a hairstyle that resembled a lioness going in for the kill.

Sure enough, she went for a kiss on the lips as she neared. I borrowed one of her old moves and tilted my head at the last second, giving her my cheek instead.

She looked startled by that development, but quickly regained her composure. "It was wonderful of you to call, Harrison. I've missed you."

"I need to talk to you." I took a deep breath, then said, "You've been to At Wick's End before you visited me here the other day, haven't you?"

Her gaze shot downward for an instant, a sure sign she was about to lie. "I don't know what you're talking about. I'd never heard of this place before then."

"Don't lie, Becka, it gives you wrinkles. Somebody saw you here arguing with Belle just before she died."

Becka's soft cooing voice turned into a shriek. "How could you think that I could have possibly done anything to that old woman. You told me it was an accident."

"So you admit you were here before?"

Becka shrugged. "I don't know who's been gossiping about me, but it's true. You should have been a partner in this place. I tried to tell her that, but she wouldn't listen."

I ran my hands through my hair. "Back up and slow down. How did you even find out about this place, and my relationship with Belle?"

"I was looking for a present for a wedding shower, and I thought a candle might be nice, one that was personalized. When I saw your aunt's name, I casually asked if you two were related. She told me you were, and I let her know how you were just getting by hand-to-mouth."

"Is that what the argument was about?" I asked coldly. I had no trouble believing Becka would butt into something that was none of her business.

"It wasn't like that, Harrison. You deserved better, don't you see that?"

"How did Belle react when you ambushed her?"

Becka said, "She had a fit. In fact, she said it wasn't any of my business. We had a few words, and I left without a candle and never came back."

I said, "Is there any way to pin down where you were the Sunday before last?"

"Sunday? I was out of town from Thursday to Tuesday on business. Why are you asking me that?" She suddenly realized where I was going. "You actually believe I could have had something to do with her accident? Harrison, I was just trying to help you."

"You had no right," I said.

Becka snapped, "Why not? You wouldn't have done anything about it, and somebody had to." Her voice eased somewhat. "I was just doing it for you. For us, really."

"You shouldn't have, and I mean that." I glanced at my watch. "You're going to have to leave, Becka, I'm opening the store in a few minutes."

"You're throwing me out? I can't believe that."

I held the door open for her. "I don't think you have any choice. Good-bye. And Becka? I do mean good-bye. Our future's all in the past."

She stalked past me, taking a stab at spiking my foot with those deadly heels, but I sidestepped her just in time. She snipped, "You'll call me. I know it and you know it."

"Don't hold your breath waiting by the phone," I said as she stormed off.

Heather was just opening up The New Age, privy to all that had been said outside. She had Esmeralda tucked under one arm. As Becka raced off in her car, Heather said, "You have a real way with the ladies, Harrison. Smooth."

I smiled. "What can I say? It's a gift." I walked over, offered a hand slowly to Esme, then rubbed her head gently. She responded with a soft purr.

"My, you two really bonded while you were roommates," Heather said.

"Let's just say we came to a mutual understanding."

Heather glanced at her watch and said, "You've got a

few minutes before you open. Why don't you come in for the grand tour?"

"That sounds great, but I can't stay long," I said as I followed her inside.

Her shop was nothing like I expected. I'd imagined a dark, gloomy place full of tarot cards and incense, heavy tapestries and beads everywhere. Instead, the store was bright and cheerful, with displays of stones, portable personal pyramids, books and pamphlets neatly on display. There were desktop waterfalls, mini-Zen gardens and polished steel balls filling out the shelves, and the place was friendlier and more inviting than I'd dreamed possible.

Heather had been watching my reaction, waiting for a comment. "You have a great shop," I said as I picked up a piece of quartz crystal. "Where do you get your stuff?"

"I get those from Hiddenite," she said. "They honestly do have healing power. Some folks swear by magnets, but I'm a crystal fan myself."

"Where's the incense," I asked.

Heather laughed. "I don't carry it, I'm allergic. That's why I don't spend much time in your candle shop. Oh, you've got to see this." Heather retrieved a candle from near the register and held it out to me. It was pale blue, with stones floating within the wax. "It's beautiful," I said as I handed it back to her.

"Belle made it for me. Isn't it cool the way she stuck the stones into the wax?"

"Actually, the stones are laid in the mold first, then the wax is poured in around them."

"You're becoming quite the expert," she said.

"I never realized before just how many ways there were to make candles. I've just started learning two methods, and there are a ton more to experiment with. Purely by accident, I think I've found my calling."

"It wasn't entirely by accident. Belle wanted you to have At Wick's End."

"What makes you say that? Did she ever say anything about her plans to you?"

Heather said, "No, but it was in her will, wasn't it?"

"Yes. Of course." I looked around and asked, "So where does Esme hang out during the day?"

"Are you kidding? The princess has her own pillow beside the cash register. It's like she's watching over the store all the time. Harrison, if you're interested, I've got a friend whose cat just had kittens."

"No thanks, I have no desire to add a roommate to my place."

She said, "Are you sure?"

I said, "I'm positive, but I'd be happy to baby-sit Esmeralda any time you need me to."

Heather grinned. "Just give me time, I'll make a cat person out of you yet."

"I'd say they were born, not made, wouldn't you? I think for now I'll settle for having one feline friend." I glanced at my watch. "I'd love to stay and chat, but I've got to open the shop."

"Come back any time, Harrison."

IT WAS A quiet morning, but I managed to sell a few things before Eve was scheduled to arrive.

It was nearly noon when Heather came into the shop. "Harrison, I need a favor. Could I borrow your old truck for a while?"

Now what in the world could I say to that?

Fifteen

HEATHER said, "Ordinarily I'd never ask, but I've got a new shipment of quartz from Hiddenite I need to pick up, and I'm afraid it's too heavy for my car."

"Don't they deliver?" I asked, stalling for time so I could figure out what to do. If I said no without a valid reason, it would certainly put Heather off. On the other hand, could she be testing me? If she'd been the one to tamper with the brake lines, she might be checking to see if I'd found the problem.

She admitted, "They'll bring my order here, but it costs twice as much, and honestly, I can't afford to stock them that way."

I asked, "So what about your store? Are you shutting it down while you go?"

"No, Mrs. Quimby came in a few minutes ago, and things are kind of slow right now." She hesitated, then added, "Never mind, Harrison. I shouldn't have asked."

"No, I don't mind, really. Tell you what. Why don't you take Belle's Ford? I just put gas in it."

Heather said, "The old Dodge is fine. Really, I don't want to take a chance messing up Belle's truck. She used to fuss at me all the time about my rocks. We had an arrangement where I'd borrow her truck, then gas it up when I got back." Heather sighed, then added, "She wouldn't take any payment from me, but she would let me buy her a pizza every now and then. Hey, I might even make an offer on your Dodge if I like it. The last thing in the world you need are two pickup trucks."

There was no way to get out of this without sounding like a nut. A sudden thought occurred to me. I could use the situation as a test for her. "Fine. Here are the Dodge keys. Have a safe trip."

Did her eyebrows raise a fraction at that? It had happened so quickly, I couldn't be sure.

Eve came in as Heather was leaving, and I called out, "I'll be right back," to her as Heather disappeared. I couldn't let her take the truck, not knowing that the brake lines had been tampered with, but I did want to see how far she'd go. I followed behind her, staying back, ready to stop her if she even put the key in the door.

She was two steps away when her cell phone rang. After a brief conversation, she turned abruptly on her heel, and caught me, dead to rights, following her.

"Harrison, what are you doing?"

"Eve came in to relieve me," I said walking toward the Ford. "I figured I'd go out and grab a bite to eat. I thought you were going after your rocks."

"I've changed my mind. Here are your keys."

"Are you sure? I honestly don't mind you taking one of the trucks," I said.

"You don't have two hours to kill right now, do you?"

I said, "I'm sorry, I don't feel right about leaving Eve that long. She just came in."

Heather looked disappointed by the news. "Don't worry, I'll get them another time. Hey, I've got an idea. Why don't you go with me next time you take a day off? It could be a fun field trip. To be honest with you, I hate going alone.

My supplier's kind of creepy, and when I go by myself he makes me really uncomfortable. That call was from a girl-friend who was supposed to go with me, but she bailed out at the last second. Belle even used to ride along with me from time to time."

"I'll make time to go with you next week. I promise," I said as I grabbed the truck keys out of her hand. "Want to grab a bite to eat with me?" I asked.

"I'd better not. I'm feeling guilty for leaving Mrs. Quimby alone. She's got a cold."

"Another time, then," I said as she walked back to her shop.

I honestly doubted that Heather had been testing me, though she'd done nothing to remove herself from my sus-pect list. The means and opportunity were there, but my problem with her was the same as with everyone else.

I couldn't for the life of me come up with a motive for Belle's murder. The only thing I knew in my gut was that her death had been no accident. And someone had their sights on me for their next victim.

I DECIDED TO go get some pizza, but April May wasn't at A Slice of Heaven. After lunch, I got back to the shop to find Eve in an uproar. "There you are. I was almost ready to call the police."

"What happened? Were we robbed?"

"No, of course not, don't be so melodramatic, Harrison." She pointed to the shelves and I saw Mrs. Jorgenson stand-ing there, studying a book on candlemaking.

I whispered, "What does she want?"

"She wouldn't tell me. She insisted on speaking only with you."

"I'd better go see what's going on, then." I wondered if she'd gotten another warning telephone call, or if the killer might have tried something even more direct.

I walked over to Mrs. Jorgenson and said, "We don't have a lesson scheduled for today."

"No, but I wanted your opinion about something. Pardon me for just dropping in like this."

"You're always welcome here, you should know that," I said. "Where did you get that?" I asked her, noticing the elegant taper in her hand.

"I wanted you to see it for yourself," she said as she held it out to me for inspection. I took the candle from her, looked at the smooth seemed edge, the carefully rolled body and the tight seating of the wick.

"So," she asked, waiting for my pronouncement. "What do you think?"

I studied it a moment longer, then said, "Well, we don't normally take candles to sell on consignment, but we might be able to find room for yours on the shelf."

Her delight was evident, though she tried to hide it. "Posh. I don't want to market it. I was just curious about your opinion."

"I heartily approve. If you'd like more practice rolling candles, we can have another lesson, but frankly, I don't think you need it."

"No, I believe I've grasped the basics. Is it time to pour yet?"

I rubbed my hands together. "You bet. I'm dying to get to it."

Sixteen

AFTER Mrs. Jorgenson was gone, Eve looked as if she were ready to cry. I said, "Don't worry, we'll live to fight another day. She's excited about the next phase in her curriculum."

Eve didn't have a chance to respond, as another customer came in, but the relief on her face was evident.

After I rang the sale up, I was ready to dig back into my books and start boning up on candle-pouring techniques.

Eve mentioned casually, "By the way, you had a visitor while you were at lunch."

I couldn't imagine Becka coming back, not after our last scene. "Who was it?"

"That attorney fellow."

"Cragg? What did he want?"

Eve said, "No, the one who used to have Markum's office; Belle's attorney, Lucas Young. Honestly, that man used to flirt shamelessly with me."

I had to fight my grin. "Did he want anything in particular, or was he here asking you out on a date?"

"Harrison, I don't find that at all amusing. Actually, he

seemed more interested in speaking with you than with me. I'm sure he'll be back."

Fighting to hide my grin, I said, "Maybe he really came by to see you, but he lost his nerve at the last minute."

"Bite your tongue. He was here for you, but I imagine we'll see him again soon. The man apparently has nothing better to do than to hover around Wick's End."

"Then I don't have to worry about calling him back, do I?" A man walked into the shop, and I turned to Eve and asked, "Do you want this customer, or shall I take him?"

"By all means, be my guest," she said.

AFTER ANOTHER LONG day, I was happy to head up to my apartment and lock the world out on the other side. I was beginning to realize that living on-site was a mixed blessing. It made the commute a breeze, but unfortunately, it also meant that I was there around the clock, good or bad, whenever anyone took the notion to see me.

Belle's sanctuary on the roof began to make more and more sense. I thought about going up to the skyline retreat, but one glance out the window told me it wouldn't be the best time to be outdoors. It was starting to rain, and the breeze was stirring up. In the distance, there was a hint of thunder rumbling in the air. From the look of things, the weather wouldn't be settling down anytime soon.

I had no desire to face the world though. I turned off the ringer on my phone, ate a quick sandwich, then curled up on the couch to read. It wasn't Dame Agatha this time, as much as I would have loved to rejoin her in Miss Marple's garden. I took the reference books I'd brought with me from the shop downstairs and started pouring over the texts. The bank deposit was still in its bag beside me, but in all honesty, I didn't have the heart or the desire to fight the coming storm or my weariness. I'd drop it off tomorrow before the shop opened, and Eve would be none the wiser.

At least it wasn't in danger of being stolen where it was.

I lit Belle's candle to give me inspiration as I read. After spending two hours with the books studying all of the things that could go wrong with a wax pour, I was beginning to be astounded that they ever turned out well. It still amazed me that candles could burn with dyes, fragrances, blocks of other waxes, even hard objects imbedded in them. I remembered how the wax would have swallowed up my first shell on my initial attempt at pouring, and realized suddenly what a wonderful hiding place the inside of a candle would be.

On a whim, I picked up Belle's last candle and turned it over, not really expecting to find anything there.

At first I didn't see anything out of the ordinary in the red bottom, but there was something about the way the light struck it that caught my eye. Was there a small square of wax that was lighter than the rest? I carried it closer to one of the floor lamps and studied it more carefully. Indeed, what was once hidden was now suddenly revealed. Belle had buried something within the mold. But why had she hidden it so carefully instead of making it a prominent part of the candle?

There was only one way to find out. Whispering a prayer asking for forgiveness, I took a hammer and screwdriver and started breaking up the last candle my great-aunt would ever pour on this earth.

THE SCREWDRIVER IN my hand clattered to the floor as I found a small tightly wrapped packet imbedded within the candle's base. What in the world was it doing there, where it had no right to be? My hands were shaking as I carefully unwrapped the package.

To my utter amazement, a twinkling diamond the size of my thumbnail tumbled out.

Now what was I going to do? My first instinct was to call Sheriff Coburn, but the way he'd been treating me lately, he'd probably claim it represented Belle's life savings and then try to tell me that she'd been afraid of banks. That wasn't fair, I knew he had more pressing worries than solving what he honestly believed to be an accidental death, but I still wasn't sure what finding the diamond really meant. It was pretty clear that Belle had uncovered evidence that someone near her had stolen the diamonds and killed the jewelry-store owner, but I was no closer to knowing who it was than the police were. What I did know, once and for all, was that Belle had been killed for what she knew. No one could claim that she'd tumbled off that ladder by accident. But who was the culprit? Clearly it had to be someone around River's Edge. That was as far as Belle's sphere of acquaintances reached.

There was only one way to find out for sure who the murderer was. I had to set a trap and see who walked into it. After I had a better idea who had committed the robbery and two homicides, I'd call Coburn and turn the evidence all over to him, including the diamond. After all, I wasn't trying to be a hero. I was just trying to find out who had murdered my great-aunt.

I knew that the diamond in my hand had to be the reason for the recent break-ins at River's Edge. Someone wanted it badly enough to trash my great-aunt's apartment and then ransack the lockers searching for it. I had to give Belle credit; no one but a candlemaker would think to look inside a candle itself.

The only problem was, now that I had it, what in the world was I going to do with it?

I STARED AT the shattered remnants of Belle's candle for nearly an hour as a plan formed in my mind. There had to be something, some way I could use my discovery to flush out Belle's killer.

Suddenly the apartment felt too crowded and confining. I needed room to pace. I walked out into the hallway, strolled up and down the carpet as I thought about what I could do. Maybe it would help to talk to someone else, to gain a little perspective. I paused at Markum's door, knocked twice, then put my ear to it.

No response, nor was there a sound coming from inside. Either he was ducking someone, or the salvage man truly was not in.

I went back to the apartment and studied the ruined shards of Belle's candle. How could I make this work for me? Then it hit me. I knew exactly what I had to do.

I looked carefully down the hallway before I headed down the stairs, just in case anyone was there. I wanted to keep a low profile going into At Wick's End. It wouldn't do to have my plans spoiled by someone watching me.

FOUR HOURS LATER I had the new candle poured. I was admiring my work when I sneezed again. It wasn't caused by the scent I'd used in pouring the candle though. I was coming down with a cold. I had been forced to guess at the exact size of the candle, since many of the molds we had were similar, though not identical, but I figured the killer wouldn't be able to tell the difference either. Matching the color was a little harder, adding a little bit of red dye at a time to the melted wax, then checking a drop on waxed paper to see the true final result. I had a chip of Belle's candle as a test piece, so the match ended up being much closer than I had expected. Since my nose was clogged, I wasn't sure how much scent to add, but I put in a modest amount of cinnamon and hoped it was enough.

I now had a nearly perfect match to Belle's candle, with one important exception. I'd found a plastic jewel used to embellish candles similar to the genuine one in Belle's effort, and I made sure one edge of it was touching the mold when I poured the wax. Belle's hiding place had been flawless, but I actually wanted everyone to see that something was in there.

I WAS JUST checking the results of the second part of my plan when Eve walked up outside the candle shop the next morning.

"Harrison, I just put that display up last week. Why did you replace it already?"

I pointed to the window. "I wanted to show off what I've been learning. Do you like it?"

"It's a fitting tribute, putting Belle's candle there." I'd put my substitute at the end of the line, clearly marking the date Belle had made it for the killer's benefit. The display showed the progression of the pouring of a candle, from a chunk of wax and some dye near a double-boiler, then on to the molds, wicks and sealers along with a careful scattering of rocks and shells, and finally to the finished product.

It was as clear as I could make the progression Belle went through to hide that diamond, but the beauty of it was that only the killer would see the true meaning behind it.

Eve walked inside and peered closely into the display. As she started to pick up the candle, she said, "What's that on the edge of the candle? How unlike Belle to be so careless with her placement."

I stopped her and said, "I've got it just the way I want it. Belle was probably just in a hurry. Hey, it happens to the best of us. Are you ready to get started on our day?"

"I'm ready," she said as her gaze lingered on the candle itself. Was she studying the red candle out of curiosity, or did she suddenly realize what Belle had done? Eve would certainly bear watching over the next few hours, along with everyone else who stepped inside At Wick's End.

I'D BEEN EXPECTING something to happen early on, and I found myself on edge as I watched the access to the window display. Millie came by around ten-thirty. "Nice window, you'all."

"Thanks," I said. "Who's minding the store?"

"We had a lull so I locked the café up. I wanted to try this new recipe for my pumpkin doughnuts on you. It's getting to be that time of year again. Would you two mind taking a taste and telling me what you think?"

Eve said, "I'd love to. Just a nibble, though."

Millie's response was to hand her an entire doughnut, just after she handed one to me.

I said, "Hey, how do you know I wanted one?"

She just smiled. "We haven't known each other all that long, but I think I know you better than that."

I said, "I wish I had the willpower to say no just to prove you wrong, but I can't. They smell too good."

It was wonderful, nothing short of perfection as I bit into the doughnut. I pretended to take my time, carefully considering all aspects of the doughnut's bouquet, texture and taste.

Eve said, "It's really rather good."

Millie turned to me. "Harrison, what do you think?"

"Honestly? It's too soon to tell. I don't suppose you have another I might try, just to compare the uniformity of the product?"

She handed me another doughnut with a smile on her face. "You scamp. Thanks for trying it."

"Millie, I'll be your taste-tester any time."

Heather came by half an hour later. If she noticed the window, she didn't mention it. "Harrison, I've got another picnic ready. Care to join me?"

I almost turned her down, since I wanted to watch that window. But couldn't I see the front of the store from the steps? And if someone reached in to grab my bait, I'd be there in time to catch the culprit red-handed.

"Okay, but I can't stay long," I said.

As we walked out of the candle shop, I asked, "What do you think of our new display window? I just finished it this morning."

She studied it a few moments, then said, "You know, Belle was always after me to learn how to make candles, but I kept putting her off. Do you think you might be able to find the time to teach me someday?"

"Absolutely. I'll even give you my River's Edge discount." It appeared that my candlemaking display was lost on her as a clue to Belle's clever hiding place.

As we walked down to the steps where we'd eaten

before, Heather produced two homemade turkey clubs and offered me a Sprite.

I said, "I'm going to have to take you somewhere fancy to make up for this."

She said, "Sometimes I get so tired of eating alone. Having your company is nice."

"So who's watching The New Age? Is Mrs. Quimby working this afternoon?"

"No, at the moment Esmeralda is my only employee. She should do just fine on her own though. She's very competent, you know."

"So you've trained her to run the cash register and answer the telephone too?"

Heather grinned. "That wasn't the toughest part. It turns out that making change gives her a headache."

"She's in good company." The entire time we ate, I kept my vigil on the window, waiting for a hand to swoop in and take the candle. A very real part of me hoped it wasn't Eve, but she probably had more reason to wish Belle harm than anyone else, especially if my great-aunt had confided her intent to give me the business instead of her.

"Harrison, is something wrong?" Heather asked.

"No, why?" I asked, keeping my gaze on the store.

"You seem distracted." She paused, then suddenly said, "I bet I know what it is. It's about the Dodge, isn't it?"

"What about the Dodge?"

She looked down at her sandwich. "Harrison, it's not that I was ashamed of driving it or anything. That's not why I changed my mind. I just couldn't bear the thought of going there alone. Honest."

"It sounds like you've got every reason in the world to avoid that place when you're by yourself," I said. "I understand completely."

"I'm glad."

After we finished our meal, Heather asked, "Would you like to take a walk along the riverbank? It's really beautiful this time of year."

"I'd like to, I honestly would, but I can't leave At Wick's End right now."

"I shouldn't leave my store either," she said with her head bowed slightly. "Another time, then."

"I promise."

I glanced over to check on the candle when I walked back into the shop, just in case I'd missed something. It was still there, crying out for attention. The display had to work. I didn't know any other way to catch the killer. I just had to accept the fact that it might take longer than I'd hoped for the culprit to show up.

WE HAD A steady flow of customers coming in and out for the rest of the day, buying the gamut from basic kits to some of our most sophisticated and expensive molds. If I'd been focusing just on our income, it would have been a banner week even without Mrs. Jorgenson's cash infusion a couple of days before. I found as time went by, I was referring fewer and fewer customers to Eve and was handling their requests myself. It felt good, growing in competence, but that blasted candle in the window took away every ounce of joy from the experience.

Finally, Eve commented on my state of mind. "Well, all I can say is that I'd hate to see you when the receipts were low if this is how you act on a good day."

"What? Sorry, I was thinking about something else."

"Obviously. Care to share what's on your mind with a harmless old woman?"

I pretended to look wildly around the store. "Is there one still here? I thought everyone left but us."

She smiled briefly. "Millie was right, you are a rascal, Harrison."

"I believe she accused me of being a scamp," I said, matching her smile.

"They both fit you." She glanced at the clock. "If you'd like, I'd be happy to make today's deposit for you. I know it's out of your way, given your commute upstairs. I don't mind, really."

I suddenly remembered yesterday's deposit, still on my couch. If I let Eve take it, I'd have to admit I'd neglected to do it yesterday. "I'll take care of it myself. It gives me an excuse to get out for a little while."

"Are you certain? I'm happy enough to do it, just as long as you don't make a habit of it."

"I appreciate the offer, but I've got it covered. Go on home. It was a good day."

She paused at the door, looked back at me and said, "Harrison, I really do like the window. It's the most fitting tribute to Belle I could imagine."

"Well, she never did like much of a fuss. Hopefully this would have made her smile."

"No doubt about it," Eve said as she left.

I locked up behind her, disappointed that my ploy hadn't worked.

I'd just have to come up with some other way to flush the killer out.

There was no way I was going to let Belle's murderer get away, now that I knew what had really happened.

Seventeen

As I drove to the bank in Belle's truck, I thought about my list of suspects, and the likelihood that any of them were involved in Belle's death as well as the murder/theft at the jewelry store.

Eve might have had a reason to kill Belle in a fit of anger. After all, she had fully expected to take over At Wick's End, and Belle had robbed her of that. But the jeweler? Hardly. Heather had no reason to kill Belle or the jewelry store owner, but she had acted rather oddly about the Dodge truck. Somehow I thought Markum would have found a way to commit the robbery and cover it up without anyone being the wiser. He seemed too competent to leave a string of bodies behind him. Pearly Gray might have had his own reasons for the initial theft, but again, he had the same air of proficiency that made me doubt he'd do such a bad job of it. Gary Cragg, the attorney, had wanted to buy the property from me, just as he had tried with Belle. Was it grounds enough for murder, and where did the robbery come into the picture? Was he planning to use the proceeds from the theft to buy the property? Becka had a temper, one of the reasons we'd parted, and she certainly could have gotten angry enough to confront Belle. In that case, it would have been in the heat of passion, not giving Belle time to hide the diamond, now safely tucked away in my front pocket. That left Millie, a woman I couldn't see harming anyone, and Lucas Young, Belle's estate attorney. He knew, better than anyone else in the world, what Belle's provisions were for tying up the property for five years. I couldn't see him committing murder either.

That left one possibility that was too outlandish for me to accept, that Belle had actually died of an accident, and that diamond had absolutely no significance whatsoever other than Belle's retirement plan. That would likely be Sheriff Coburn's take on things, but I wasn't buying it.

I'd never been a big fan of coincidences. Not when it came to murder.

I HALF-EXPECTED the shop door to be burgled when I got back, but everything was still as I'd left it in At Wick's End, with the candle still holding down its corner of the display.

My plan to flush out the killer had been a wash. It was time to get back to the business of candlemaking. After all, that was where my living was coming from for at least the next five years. I'd have to come up with some other way to trap Belle's killer.

MY WATER BATH for Belle's substitute candle had worked out fine, leaving me with a candle unmarred by the pinpricks, striations, cracks or bubbles the books all warned about. But I didn't feel competent enough to teach the technique yet. I knew I still needed a great deal of practice before I was ready for my next session with Mrs. Jorgenson.

I was just starting to pour another candle to be sure I knew what I was doing when there was an urgent pounding at the front door. Without even realizing I was still carrying the jug of hot wax in my hand, I walked up front to see who was trying to get my attention so late after closing.

It was Lucas Young, no doubt checking up again to see how I was adapting to my new life. He'd be disappointed when he found that Eve was already gone for the day.

I opened the door and said, "Come in, Lucas. What brings you to At Wick's End?"

"I'm glad you're still here, Harrison. I was out this way this evening and saw your window display. It's quite touching, actually, a fine tribute to your aunt. Great-aunt," he corrected automatically.

"Thanks. I wanted to do something to mark her passing, and I thought it would be appropriate." The window was certainly getting a great deal of attention, there was no doubt about that.

"In fact," he continued. "I'd like to buy that particular candle from you. It would give me a keepsake to remember Belle by. She was one of the finest women I ever knew."

"Sorry, but it's not for sale," I said as a chill ran through me.

He wasn't about to give up that easily. "Come now, you're just starting a business brand-new to you. I know what your financial situation looks like, Harrison. Surely you've got enough of your own memories to part with this one object. I'm willing to be quite generous with you."

"I'm sorry, but this one's kind of special."

Then I knew. Lucas Young was behind it all. Things started to click in my mind, coincidences coming together that didn't make sense any other way. His constant appearances around the shop, his familiarity with the building since he'd been the tenant in Markum's old office at one time, and the fact that he'd been the only one who'd had a key to Belle's apartment legally as her executor; there were too many coincidences for my taste. I studied him, wondering what his motive could be, wishing I'd armed myself with a baseball bat or something to defend myself with. All I had was a pot of wax.

Hot wax. Maybe, if it came to that, it could work.

"I really must insist," the attorney said, reaching into his jacket pocket. I could see the outline of something bulky there, and there was no doubt in my mind he was going for a gun.

It was time to stop playing detective before he did anything I'd live to regret. I had no desire to face a man with a gun when all I had was a pitcher of hot wax. Before Young could finish that motion, I said, "I had no idea she meant that much to you. Of course you can have it."

He eased his hand back out of his pocket, and instead reached for his wallet. "Would a hundred dollars be sufficient?"

"That would be fine," I said.

The attorney took the candle after handing me the money. As he walked toward the door, I eased my grip on the wax. Once Young was outside, I'd call Sheriff Coburn and tell him all I knew. Let him take the risks. After all, that's why he was the sheriff and I was the candlemaker.

The attorney held the candle tightly as he stopped near the door, then slid the dead bolt in place instead of walking out.

"What's wrong," I asked. "Did you forget something?"

"No, but you did. I happened to smell this candle in Belle's apartment when I broke in, and it had the distinct aroma of cinnamon. This one smells like clove."

Blast it all, I'd added the wrong scent! I was coming down with a cold, so the different aroma had been lost on me as I made the duplicate, and in my rush to finish the candle, I must have grabbed the wrong bottle of essence.

Young said, "That can mean only one thing. You must know," he said, this time pulling the gun all the way out of his jacket pocket.

There are times I just hate being right.

"I don't know what you're talking about," I said, trying to stall him long enough to come up with some kind of plan to get myself out of a pretty bad situation.

"Give it up, Harrison. You wouldn't take the bait on the

Dodge, so I decided to delay killing you until I could come up with another *accident.* No time for that now. It looks like you're going to have to die in a robbery attempt. A pity really, since we both know how little you actually make here."

"But why kill me at all," I asked, wondering if I could throw the wax at him and get out of the way of the shot in time.

"I'm afraid that's been my final option from the beginning. You see, there was something you weren't meant to know, an additional codicil to Belle's will just in case you refused to leave. Your great-aunt didn't know about it either, for that matter. I added a little proviso that turned the estate over to its executor if you decided to quit or if something happened to you before the one-year anniversary of Belle's death. You didn't stand a chance."

"So when you found out you couldn't run me off, you decided to tamper with my brakes."

Again Young looked surprised by the conclusion. "I must say, Harrison, I believe I underestimated you. I worked in a garage when I was an undergraduate, so it was easy enough to do. I purposely neglected to mention Belle's truck to you, but evidently someone couldn't keep their mouth shut. I had the perfect setup, but you somehow found me out."

"I was on the roof when you were sabotaging my truck," I said. "I saw you run away, but it was too dark and too far away for me to see who you were. I just don't get why you'd stoop to murder. You did all this so you could convert River's Edge into a lawyer's complex like Cragg was going to do?"

Young laughed. "Hardly. I have more ambitious plans. What wonderful condominiums these will make. I'll be able to pay off my gambling debts and have a steady income to indulge my hobby." Then I remembered Pearly saying that he'd seen Young on his way to the racetrack in West Virginia.

I said, "Listen, I know I don't have a chance, you're

holding all the cards. Just tell me one thing before you do anything rash." I needed to appeal to his ego if I had the slightest chance of getting out of this alive.

"A last request," he said. "How dramatic."

"Why did you choose River's Edge to hide the diamonds you stole?"

"Thanks for reminding me," he said. "Where's the one Belle found?"

"I'll answer you if you answer me," I said. What did I have to lose? At least I wouldn't die of curiosity.

"I used to lease Markum's office, I don't know if you're aware of that or not. There's a floor safe up there he doesn't know about, so I figured it would be a perfect place to hide something important. The only problem was that I dropped the bag of diamonds in the hallway in my haste. Belle saw me as I was leaving the building the night of the robbery, but I made up an excuse about coming to the complex to see her. She would have bought it too, if I hadn't lost one of the diamonds. She decided to confront me the next evening, and I knew I had to do something. In a very real way, it was self-defense. One quick shove was all it took. Then it was simply a matter of staging the accident downstairs. I would have been home free if I could have only found that blasted diamond. I thought I covered my tracks by killing the jeweler, but Belle suddenly became another loose end."

"So why did you kill him?"

"I handled Bleeker's business affairs along with that cluck Ann Marie, so I knew the way his security system operated. I needed something to pay off my creditors, though it wasn't enough to satisfy them completely. They gave me quite a bit less than top dollar for the diamonds, but I wasn't in any position to complain. It was surprisingly easy to dispatch the jeweler, he was extraordinarily careless. Kudos to you, Harrison, you figured this out with the sparsest of clues."

"It's the only way it all made sense. Belle must have found the errant jewel and somehow tied it to you." Another thought occurred to me. "You didn't have anything to do with my deposit being robbed, did you? You did," I said as I saw him smile.

"I needed you to give up your claim to the property, Harrison, if I was going to be able to take over River's Edge. I followed you to the library and couldn't believe my good luck when you left the deposit on the front seat of the cab. It was a perfect opportunity to drive you away. But I underestimated you, didn't I? Ann Marie told me about your special client who was going to save the day, so I had to discourage her from patronizing your shop. I thought the telephone call would be enough of a threat to keep her away, but she was more determined than I thought she'd be. After that, I knew that I wasn't going to be able to scare you away from At Wick's End, so it was time to take more drastic measures."

"So you decided to mess with my brakes."

Young smiled. "I purposely didn't tell you about Belle's truck, so you'd have to drive the Dodge. I knew you'd drive it again sooner or later. The condition it's in, I doubted anyone would look twice at an accident."

"Your *accidents* are getting to be a habit for you, aren't they?"

Young shook his head. "Belle didn't have to die. If she'd only minded her own business, I never would have had to take action. She was going to turn me in. Hiding that diamond in the candle was a stroke of brilliance, I have to credit her for that. She shouldn't have confronted me first though. Can you imagine, she wanted me to have the opportunity to turn myself in before she did. That was her last mistake."

I'd heard all I needed to hear. "And you've made yours," I said as I threw the hot wax at him, hoping to burn his face with it for killing my great-aunt.

He threw his hands up automatically to defend himself and caught the sizzling wax square on. There was no way he could hold a gun with the burns, so I picked the weapon up and trained it on him as I dialed Sheriff Coburn's number.

* * *

THE NEXT MORNING, after very little sleep, and troubled at that, we held an impromptu meeting at The Crocked Pot with most of the tenants at River's Edge, including Markum.

"What I want to know is how he slipped back into my office without my keys," Markum said.

Pearly said, "I hate to admit this, but I've come to the conclusion he made copies of mine. I keep a master set, it's required by the fire marshal. Young must have absconded with my set, duplicated them, then returned them without me being aware of it. He hovered around here quite a bit, you know."

Heather said, "Harrison, you should never have tackled him on your own. You could have been killed."

I smiled at her, then at Eve. "I had the perfect defensive weapon with me. That wax is hot!"

Eve said, "I told you all along, you have to be careful with it." She glanced at the clock. "I'm so happy it's all turned out for the best, but it's almost time to open our shop."

I got up to follow, and Eve added, "Why don't you come in later? You had an active night. Go up to your apartment and get some rest."

"Maybe I'll do that," I said.

Markum said, "Well, I've got to head out too. I need to move my desk." He looked at Pearly and asked, "Do you have time to give me a hand?"

"Absolutely," Pearly said.

That left Millie, Cragg, Heather and me. Cragg glanced at his watch and said, "I've got to get over to the courthouse. I'm defending Lucas Young."

I said, "No offense, but I hope you lose."

He shrugged. "The accused is entitled to the best defense possible."

"You mean that their money can buy," Millie added, loud enough for Cragg to hear on his way out.

"Now what can I do for you two," she asked. "More coffee? How about some pumpkin doughnuts? I just made a new batch."

"If I drink any more coffee, I'll never be able to take a nap."

Heather said, "Who are you kidding? If At Wick's End is open, you're going to be there. That's where you belong, Harrison."

"It is, isn't it?"

As I walked to the candle shop, I found myself wishing I'd had the chance to thank Belle for my new life. She'd given me a great trust, leaving River's Edge, and At Wick's End in particular, to me.

I made a solemn promise to her that I'd do my best to live up to that trust.

I walked back in and Eve was looking frantic. "Thank goodness I found you."

"You couldn't have been looking that hard, I was still at The Crocked Pot."

Eve said, "You don't understand. Mrs. Jorgenson just called. She wants her first lesson on pouring candles this morning, and no one else will do."

After facing down a killer the night before, I was pretty sure I could handle Mrs. Jorgenson.

After all, pouring candles was my new specialty.

Belle's Snickerdoodle Cookies

This is a longtime favorite of my family.
These cookies are great right out of the oven,
but they're just as tasty right out of the freezer.

2¾ cups sifted all-purpose flour
2 teaspoons cream of tartar
1 teaspoon baking soda
A dash of salt
1 cup butter or margarine, creamed
1½ cups sugar
2 eggs
3 tablespoons sugar
3 teaspoons cinnamon

Combine the flour, cream of tartar, baking soda and salt. Sift this mixture thoroughly, then set it aside. Cream the butter (or margarine) until fluffy, then gradually add the sugar and eggs. Stir in the dry ingredients, then chill the dough until it's cool to the touch. This makes it easier to work with. Make balls a little bigger than a quarter, then roll them in the combined cinnamon/sugar mix. Place them two inches apart on an ungreased cookie sheet and bake at 400 degrees Fahrenheit. The cookies take 8–10 minutes to bake and will be lightly browned on top.

This recipe makes about 4 dozen cookies.

Millie's Pumpkin Doughnuts

For a delightful treat on a brisk autumn day,
my family and I make these doughnuts
when the leaves start to turn.

3 cups sifted all-purpose flour
1 tablespoon baking powder
1 teaspoon baking soda
½ teaspoon salt
1 teaspoon cinnamon
1 teaspoon ground ginger
¼ cup butter or margarine, soft
¾ cup sugar
2 eggs
1 can solid pack pumpkin
⅔ cup buttermilk

Combine flour, baking powder, baking soda, salt, cinnamon and ginger; then sift and set aside. Cream butter until fluffy, then gradually add the sugar and beat until fluffy again. Beat in ¼ cup of the dry ingredients, then add pumpkin and buttermilk and mix thoroughly. Add the remaining dry ingredients and stir just until blended. Cover and refrigerate for 2 hours. Roll dough out on floured surface to ¼-inch thickness, then cut out doughnuts and holes with a 3½-inch doughnut cutter. While the doughnut cut-outs are resting, heat 4 inches of oil in a heavy large saucepan to 365 degrees Fahrenheit. Add doughnuts and holes and cook until golden brown, turning once. Drain on paper towels, then dust with powdered sugar and enjoy.

Tips for Making Beeswax Rolled Candles

Rolled candles are a great way to begin candlemaking. They are easy to make, producing a satisfying product with minimum effort. And the candles burn great too. This is an especially easy way to get started with kids.

Once you've mastered the technique of rolling a tight candle with the wax sheets, it's fun to play and experiment with cookie cutters. We make all kinds of shapes, from card-suit candles to red hearts on Valentine's Day to green Christmas tree candles in December. It's especially nice to alternate two complementary colors as you build up your cookie cutter candles. For July 4th, try stacking individual candle cut-outs with red, cream and blue waxes for a patriotic centerpiece candle.

To make a layered candle with cookie cutters, treat the wax sheet as if it were dough and cut individual thicknesses out of the colored wax you prefer. Open cutters work best here, as the wax sometimes gets stuck in the closed cutters. Build a candle with four or six layers, remembering to put the wick in the middle. Don't be afraid to press the edges of the candle together. This gives the candle a softer, more rounded look and also serves to bind the pieces together. A blow-dryer gently run over the edges can help soften the wax, just enough to further press the candle together.

Another technique we enjoy with wax sheets is rolling two diagonally trimmed pieces, alternating colors together, giving the candle a nice layered look.

To finish off your rolled projects, you can dip the bottoms in a pan of melted wax, sealing the candle and giving it a more stable base, but it's not really necessary.

The most important thing to remember when making candles is to have fun!

AUTHOR BIOGRAPHY

Tim Myers lives with his family near the Blue Ridge Mountains he loves and writes about. He is the award-winning author of the Agatha-nominated Lighthouse Inn mystery series featuring *Innkeeping with Murder, Reservations for Murder, Murder Checks Inn* and *Room for Murder,* as well as over seventy short stories. Two books in this series have been named National Bestsellers by the Independent Mystery Booksellers Association.

At Wick's End is the first in Tim's new Candlemaking mystery series, from Berkley Prime Crime. Coming next in the series will be *Burning at Both Ends,* featuring the murder of one of Harrison's tenants at River's Edge.

Tim has been a stay-at-home dad for the last twelve years, finding time for murder and mayhem whenever he can.

To learn more, visit his website at *www.timmyers.net* or contact him at timothylmyers@hotmail.com

Coming Soon

A SCRAPBOOKING MYSTERY
SCRAPBOOK TIPS INCLUDED

Keepsake Crimes

LAURA CHILDS

First in a new
series by the
author of
*The Tea Shop
Mystery* Series

Berkley Prime Crime

0-425-19074-9

LOVE MYSTERY?

From cozy mysteries to procedurals,
we've got it all. Satisfy your cravings with our monthly
newsletters designed and edited specifically for fans of who-
dunits. With two newsletters to choose from, you'll be sure to
get it all. Be sure to check back each month or sign up for
free monthly in-box delivery at

www.penguin.com

Berkley Prime Crime

Berkley publishes the premier writers of mysteries.
Get the latest on your
favorties:
Susan Wittig Albert, Margaret Coel, Earlene
Fowler, Randy Wayne White, Simon Brett, and
many more fresh faces.

Signet

From the Grand Dame of mystery,
Agatha Christie, to debut authors,
Signet mysteries offer something for every reader.

*Sign up and sleep with
one eye open!*